KEPT BRIDE

THE SECRET BRIDE SERIES - BOOK TWO

ALTA HENSLEY

Special Thank you to my editor: Kayla Robichaux and my wonderful beta readers.

Cover Design: Jay Aheer

DEDICATION

To my husband. I'll be your Kept Bride forever.

PROLOGUE
CHRISTOPHER

FLAMES IN THE SKY, SMOKE IN OUR EYES, AND blinding lights—we are no longer alone.

I thought I'd seen fear before, but nothing measures up to what I see in Ember's eyes now. She's trapped in a terror I can't save her from, though I try.

"It's okay," I shout above the sirens of the firetrucks and the police cars. "We're going to be okay." Even as I repeat the words, I don't know what "okay" looks like. "Help is here."

I hold her hand in mine as I wave down the speeding vehicles with my other.

It becomes a blur after that. So many questions, so many people, so many curious eyes looking.

We're emerging from the ashes, and yet it still feels as if the devil takes hold.

I keep waiting for Richard to march from the smoky landscape, take us both prisoner again, and the chain to never be removed.

I want a gun to defend myself but know there isn't a single police officer who will give me one.

I want to run up to the burning main house with the firefighters just so I can see the corpse of the monster, known as Richard, sizzle to ash. I want to see his death with my own eyes, but I'm also aware that is not a possibility.

For now, I have to be content that we are saved.

Saved... but not necessarily *safe*.

Because what does *safe* really mean?

1

"I DON'T KNOW HOW MANY TIMES I HAVE TO ANSWER the same questions," I say, leaning back in the metal chair, feeling it dig into my achy back. "I need to see Ember."

"Just a few more questions," Detective Jackson says. "She's still being questioned too, so if you can just be patient, we—"

"I've been patient enough," I snap. "I told you all that I know, and I also told you that Ember has to be terrified right now. She's not used to people, and I need to be by her side. It's been hours, and I'm exhausted. I don't know what more I can offer. I told you all about that psychopath, about me being chained to a goddamn wall and forced to marry his daughter. I told you every last sick detail. What more do you want from me?"

Detective Jackson looks down at his notes as if he didn't listen to a word I said and asks, "So, this Ember woman... you said she claims she's been there since she was a child?"

"Yes," I say on a heavy exhale. "She's as much a victim as I am." I stand up, place my palms on the table, and stare down the detective. "Do I need to ask for my attorney? Because I'm starting to feel that way."

Detective Jackson leans back in the chair and crosses his arms. "Do you feel there is a reason to have an attorney?"

"You tell me," I say and then look at the mirror in the room, trying to see whoever is on the other side. But instead, all I see is my reflection.

Wearing clothing they give to inmates, with matching shoes, I look like a stranger. My hair is long and hangs in my face. I look like I've lost weight while I was losing months of my life. I suppose I should be grateful for the dry clothes they gave Ember and me when we arrived, but it only reminds me of just how much of a prison I've been living in.

"Just a few more questions," Jackson pushes on.

"Unless you're going to charge me or Ember with anything, we're leaving. So please take me to her. Now."

"I understand your frustration," he says. "But the Feds just arrived and are asking Ember more questions."

"I need to see her. I need to be with her. And like I said, unless you're arresting us, I expect to be taken to her now."

Ember hadn't said a word to me since the rescue. She answered all the questions the medics asked as they tended to our wounds around our ankles caused by the chains. And although she was polite and was free with her answers, it seemed as if every syllable hurt her. I knew she hadn't spoken to a single soul other than her father, me, and Scarecrow. I knew she had to be so scared, and to be without me had to have her even more so.

I'm hating the interrogation from the police, so I can only imagine how she must be handling it.

"I'll make a deal with you," Detective Jackson says as he joins me in standing. "I'll bring you to her, but only if you can stay a little bit longer to allow the Feds to get what they want."

I know I don't have to agree to anything, since we aren't under arrest, but I also want to help put this nightmare to an end.

I nod and follow him out of the room and down the hall to another interrogation room.

When I enter, I see Ember looking so tiny and frail on a chair that seems to nearly swallow her up. Her wide eyes lock with mine, and her lower lip trembles the minute she sees me.

I rush to where she sits and kneel at her feet, looking up at her. "Hey," I say softly. "I'm here now. I'm not going to leave your side again." I take her hand, which is cold from the chill in the air of the sterile room. "Are you doing all right?"

Her eyes dart to the man in front of her and then to me. She nods. "They keep asking me about Papa Rich and Scarecrow, and—"

"I know," I interrupt as I get up and take the seat next to her. "It's almost over." I look directly into the men's eyes as they sit across from us. "Correct? Do you have what you need?"

The man looks at Detective Jackson, who motions for him to join him outside. As the two men leave the room, I position my body so I can look at Ember head-on.

Taking both her hands into mine, I say, "We're going to get out of here soon. I promise."

"And then what? Where will we go?" she asks, which makes sense. The only home she has ever known has just burned to the ground.

"I called my mother," I begin. "After nearly causing the woman to have a stroke from hearing from her *dead son*, I made arrangements."

Ember shakes her head. "I don't understand. Arrangements?"

"My mother is in Palm Springs with some of her friends for a vacation. Hearing that we're here... alive... she chartered a private plane so we can get back to New York as fast as possible. She's on her way now to pick us up."

"New York?"

"That's where I live, remember?" I prompt softly, understanding this has to be a lot for Ember to take in. "It's where we will both live now."

Her hands shake in mine, and all I want to do is sweep her up into my arms, get her as far away from Nevada and Hallelujah Junction as I can, and never speak of Papa Rich and this hell ever again. But as the detectives reenter the room, I know I can't have everything right away.

"If you don't mind, we have a couple more questions," Detective Jackson says. "This is Federal Agent Martinez."

"Go ahead," I say, deciding I will answer all the questions I can to avoid them from asking Ember. I can feel in my gut that the poor girl is reaching her max on what she can take.

"So, there are some things you both have said that don't exactly add up. You said you saw this *Papa Rich* run into the burning house?" Agent Martinez asks.

"Yes," I say as I squeeze Ember's hand in reassurance that I have this handled. "I think we've both told you this multiple times."

"No body was discovered in the house," Martinez tells us. "In fact, no bodies have been discovered anywhere in the structures."

I feel Ember's hand go limp in mine. The gut-punching news has me swallowing hard but not wanting to believe the words.

"We saw him go inside," I say. "The house was engulfed in flames."

"But you also both say you continued running and never looked back. Neither of you know if he left the house or not. Correct?"

"Papa Rich is alive?" Ember's shaky voice cuts in. A single tear falls down her face, and I don't know if it's from relief or fear.

Martinez and Jackson both glare at Ember. "You said you don't know where his friend 'Scarecrow' lives. Are you sure you've never visited or heard any details that could help us track this fellow down?"

Ember shakes her head. "He always came to us, or Papa Rich went to him without me. I know he's in the hills somewhere, and it's not exactly close. It takes all day to go back and forth from his home to Hallelujah Junction."

"Did either of you see Scarecrow during the fire?"

"No," I answer. "Are you telling us that you think Richard is still alive? Maybe hiding out with Scarecrow?"

"We're exploring all possibilities right now. All we know is there are no signs of Richard dying in the fire like you both claim."

Ember gasps and looks at me with renewed terror in her eyes. "He's going to find us. He's going to punish us. He won't give up until he does."

I run my hand over the side of her head, caressing her soft blonde locks. "Shh," I try to soothe. "He's not going to be able to find us. And *if* he's alive—*if* —then these men right here are going to find him and lock him away for life." I continue stroking her hair, trying to pet her anxiety away. "We're safe now. I promise you. We're safe."

I glare at the men, pissed that they are only adding to Ember's fear. "If he's not dead, find the sick asshole. You're both wasting time by asking us the same questions over and over."

Detective Jackson looks down at his notes and papers. "Ember, we also looked into the report you gave about how Papa Rich found you and brought you to Hallelujah Junction. The story of being picked up in a nearby town and rescuing you from your mother. We went back and looked up if there were any reports of kidnapping around that time, which there weren't necessarily. But there are records of a young girl who Child Protective Services visited in the area who suddenly turned up missing with no notice from the mother or forwarding address. The child's name was Amber

Jennings. Amber... not Ember." He takes a moment for the words to sink in. "We believe Amber Jennings is you." He pushes a file toward us. "There's a picture in there. It looks like a younger version of you."

Ember opens the file and stares down at a picture that no doubt is of her as a five-year-old. You can see the familiarity in the eyes. Such big, blue, and haunted eyes.

"Amber?" she questions more to herself than anyone else. "No, my name is Ember."

"Is that picture you?"

She nods. "But my name is Ember. Not Amber."

"Maybe now... but you were once Amber Jennings."

Tears fill her eyes, and she asks, "What about my mother? Will she know where I am now? Papa Rich told me that she'd kill me if she ever found where I was."

I reach over and close the file, feeling as if this is all too much for her. "It doesn't matter. You're Ember now. And you're safe. The past is the past. Your mother can't hurt you. No one can hurt you."

"We pulled up information on your mother, and I'm sorry to say—or maybe in your case, happy to inform you—she died thirteen years ago."

"Thirteen?" Ember parrots, and without even having to hear the words, I know what she's thinking. She's been safe for thirteen years from all the horror stories Papa Rich told her about her mother coming to hurt her if she ever discovered her location. She could have left the walls of the schoolhouse living as the ghost of Hallelujah Junction had she known the woman didn't exist anymore.

"We've also pulled up every report of missing people who have visited Hallelujah Junction with the belief that their cause of death is due to the acid pit and the old mill," Agent Martinez says. "We have found a report for a couple who matches your description of the victims you witnessed pushed into the pit." He slides over the paper with their photos on it. "Are these the people you encountered?"

I glance down and nod as I rub Ember's back. On the surface, Ember is holding it together. And maybe she is. But I can't help but feel we are walking a very dangerous tightrope, and she's about to come crashing down any second.

"We weren't aware they went to Hallelujah Junction," Detective Jackson says.

"They were trying to help us," Ember murmurs.

"As for the others," Martinez continues, "Ember, did you help your father kill those people?"

I stand up and hit my hand on the table. "That's enough! Unless you both plan to charge Ember or me with anything, we are leaving. We've been here voluntarily for long enough. My wife and I have nothing left to say unless a lawyer is present."

Ember reaches for my arm and gently pulls me down. "It's okay, Christopher. I don't mind answering." She looks at the detective and agent. "All I know is I didn't stop it."

"You *couldn't* stop it," I boom.

"And I will have to live with that and their deaths for the rest of my life," she adds.

"The man was sick!" I shout, but then lower my voice to add, "More than you can imagine. He kidnapped and had me locked in a cellar. Chained to a wall like a rabid dog. I watched as he killed that couple with zero remorse, and there was nothing I, or Ember, could do to stop it. There is absolutely no way Ember had anything to do with those deaths. Not at all. And I'm not going to sit here with my wife and allow this conversation to go in that direction. Are we clear?"

Rather than answering my demand of a question, Martinez asks, "If your father were to run and hide somewhere, where do you think he'd go? Other than this Scarecrow man, does he have any other family or friends?"

Ember shakes her head with a deep sadness in her eyes. "We had no one. We were alone. We only had each other."

"And where do you both plan to go now? If we have any more questions." Agent Martinez looks at us with zero emotion in his eyes. I want to punch the fucker. We just went through this awful ordeal, and he has the nerve to accuse *us* and question *us*.

"We'll be heading home. New York."

"I'd rather you stay in town," Detective Jackson pipes in. "In case we have any further—"

"We'll be flying out within the hour," I interrupt. "Unless I need to call my lawyer, that is."

Agent Martinez stands up, and Detective Jackson follows. Agent Martinez glances at Ember, then at me and says, "That's all for now. I'll be in contact if we have any further questions."

"Mr. Martinez," Ember calls to him as he begins to walk out of the room.

He turns to face her but doesn't answer.

"Is it possible for me to have that photo of me as a child? I don't have any photos. I don't have anything."

I am prepared to lunge for the man and rip the file with her photo right out of his hands if I have to, but luckily, he nods and hands it to her.

"Thank you," she says as she stares down at the picture I'm sure she doesn't truly even recognize.

My heart breaks for what Ember must be feeling. In a matter of hours, she has lost everything. She's been told her mother, who she has feared her entire life, is dead. She's also been told that the father she was forced to live with in captivity could now possibly be alive.

Her eyes remain on the photo as she says, "I've never been on a plane before."

The number of firsts coming up for her are sure to be staggering. All I can do is try to help her muddle through them.

"Well, the good news is, my mother insisted on a private jet, so we won't have to deal with all the crowds. It will be more comfortable too. We can have something to eat on the plane and get some sleep. You look tired." I know I sure as hell am.

Finally breaking her gaze from the picture, she looks up at me with eyes that could tell a lifetime of horrific tales. "You called me your wife," she says in a monotone voice with zero emotion on her face. A blank pallet that leaves me wondering what she's thinking.

"Because you are," I say.

I don't have the mental bandwidth to dive into what our future looks like beyond getting on a plane and getting the hell out of here. I need distance from this nightmare before I can even think. I need clean clothes, shoes that fit, and a goddamn drink. I need normalcy. I fucking need a minute where I feel ordinary.

"I'm scared," Ember admits, but I don't need to hear the words to know that she is.

I pull her up out of the chair and embrace her tight. "We're going to figure this all out. I don't have all the answers now. I don't know what happens next. But you and I will figure it out."

2

EMBER

"OH MY GOD. OH MY GOD. OH MY GOD. OH MY God," an older woman who has the same facial bone structure as Christopher says as she walks toward us, stunned with her mouth wide open. "Oh. My. God." She places her fingers on her lips as a floodgate of tears releases from her eyes. "You're alive. You are really alive. You're really here! Oh my God."

"I'm alive," Christopher says as he approaches and pulls her into a hug. "I'm alive, Mom." He looks up at the sky, then inhales deeply, closing his eyes briefly as he does.

I can't look away, even though I feel as if I'm invading their privacy by observing this twisted reunion. What it must be like to embrace a ghost.

To hold your dead son in your arms, only to feel the warmth of life and the breath of the living.

"I know I heard your voice on the phone, but to see you." His mother pulls away from the hug and looks Christopher over from head to toe. "You're really here. I can't believe you're really here. How did this happen? How?"

"There's a lot to tell you," Christopher says as he then turns away from her and reaches out his hand for me to take. "But first, I want to introduce you to Ember. She was with me in Hallelujah Junction, and we escaped together." When I cautiously approach and take his hand, he adds, "Ember, this is my mother, Louisa Davenport."

Louisa glances down at my hand intwined with her son's and then paints a smile on her face as she gives a slight nod in acknowledgement. She then reaches her hand out to me. I'd never shaken a hand before but know what to do from all my reading. It's odd to touch someone else—a complete stranger—but I want to be polite. I want Christopher's mother to like me.

"Nice to meet you, Ember," she says as she grips my hand firmly.

"Nice to meet you, Mrs. Davenport." I make eye contact with her and notice she has hazel eyes beneath very thick eyelashes against heavily gray-eyeshadowed lids. I've never worn makeup before and wonder if Louisa will someday show me how to apply it like she does.

She is still smiling, but her upper lip twitches, and her eyes seem to bore right through me. I reposition myself from one foot to the other as I feel the weight of her assessment on my shoulders pushing me down and making me feel small.

I need to escape, and yet I have no place to go. No place to run to.

I also don't want to stand on the pavement near the large jet any longer. I wish I could flee and go hide in a corner somewhere out of sight. I need to breathe someplace that is all my own, and yet I can't. I release Christopher's hand, which oddly briefly frees me from the stare of Mrs. Davenport when I do.

"You both look like prison inmates," she says with a wrinkle of her nose as if we possess an odor.

Rather than being offended, Christopher chuckles, and for the first time, I see laugh lines around his eyes and a look of genuine... glee. It's foreign to me, and that fact smacks me hard with what our reality was and what it is now.

"Fitting, since we both were in a prison of sorts for months."

I don't like Christopher referring to our life in Hallelujah Junction as a prison. I understand why he does, but it doesn't sound right. It doesn't feel right. And even though we are both dressed in clothing given to us by the police, I don't like being compared to an inmate either.

She looks at Christopher, finally breaking her searing stare on me. "Is she coming with us?"

I look at Christopher for an answer as well. Am I?

Christopher swallows hard and nods. "There's... something... that happened while I was held captive." He looks at me and places his palm on my lower back, which gives me a sense of comfort. "The man holding me there forced me to marry Ember. She's my wife, Mom. We're married."

Her fingertips flutter to her lips as her eyes widen. "Your wife? He forced you to marry? You can't be serious."

He nods. "There's a lot I have to tell you about my nightmare, but right now, Ember and I really need to get on the plane, eat something, and get some rest. I also really want to get the hell out of Nevada and never step foot in this godforsaken place again. I can tell you everything once we're in the air. I'm sure you have a lot of questions, but I could sure use a stiff drink."

I look at the jet with the door open and stairs leading up to it, beckoning us to enter. I can't imagine how something so big and what looks so heavy can possibly get in the air and not fall out of the sky.

"Ember?" Christopher prompts as he breaks me from my thoughts. "You ready?"

Without waiting for an answer, he leads me to the plane and up the stairs. His hand stays touching some part of me the entire time, and I realize just how much I need it. I cling to it. I focus on it to try to calm the flutter in my chest and tone down the ringing in my ears. My legs feel weak as I walk up every single stair, and when we enter the jet, I try not to focus on the thin metal walls that surround me. It's as if I've been swallowed up, and it suddenly seems harder to breathe.

"It's going to be just fine," he says softly from behind me. His lips are near my ear, and it takes all my might to keep walking forward to some seats he's guiding me to. "I know this is all new and maybe scary, but it's going to be fine."

"You've never flown before?" Mrs. Davenport asks as she takes one of the leather seats.

"Mom, I told you. Ember was held captive just like me. She grew up in Hallelujah Junction. Richard— the man responsible for my kidnapping—held her there since she was a young child."

I want to correct Christopher. I wasn't captive. I wasn't held there. Papa Rich is my father. Hallelujah Junction is my... *was* my home. But I remain quiet. Mrs. Davenport is glaring at me again, and I can't help but get the feeling that the woman doesn't care for me. By the way her eyes keep darting to Christopher's touch on me, I can clearly see she doesn't like him touching me one bit.

As we take our seats directly across from his mother, Christopher reaches over my lap and buckles a seat belt over me. Mrs. Davenport doesn't like seeing this either. I miss the smile she had painted on her face before. She's not even trying to hide her distaste now.

"So let me get this straight," she finally says as the plane starts to move. "The man who kidnapped you—Richard—forced you to marry Ember, who he also kidnapped?"

"Yes," Christopher says as he reaches for a shelf that stores glasses and some decanters of colored and clear liquid. He looks at me. "Do you want a drink?"

I shake my head. I worry I won't be able to hold down what is in my stomach once this plane actually lifts off into the sky.

Christopher pours his mother a drink without asking if she wants one and then pours himself one. "The man was called Richard, and he normally kills anyone who trespasses," Christopher begins. "I guess I should consider myself lucky he deemed me the one to marry his daughter... or who he considered his daughter... even though Ember is just as much a victim as I was. He made it look like I died in an accident, which sadly is how many other people actually died, and he kept me chained in the basement."

I bite the inside of my cheek to stay quiet. I'm not a victim. I don't like being referred to as one, but I also don't feel it's appropriate to correct Christopher in front of his mother. Instead, I look out the window at the passing scenery and try to not let the panic setting in overtake me.

"They told me you died while taking pictures. That you fell to your death in an old mining pit of acid. I had no idea. I just assumed that— I had no idea." She shakes her head and breathes deeply. "What kind of sick man would do this?"

"There is no way you could have known I was still alive."

"And you both escaped? Where is this Richard now?" she asks as she takes a long swallow of her drink. She leaves red lipstick marks on the glass, and I am once again reminded of the makeup I lack.

I wonder what this woman must think of me.

I feel plain and simple.

I also feel dirty and wrong.

I'm out of place, and I don't belong.

"I waited until the perfect time. We started a fire that burned down the town. We thought Richard died in the fire, but the police just told us that might not be the case. Regardless, we are free from him forever. If he is alive, he's a wanted man and will have to hide in holes until someone eventually finds him."

"I think I'll get us some security just in case," she says as if it's just as simple as that to make any threat of Papa Rich go away.

"If that makes you feel better," he agrees as he reaches for my hand and holds it in his.

We take off into the air, and my belly drops and then flips. A cold sweat covers me, and I instantly want off the plane. I want to go home. I want the schoolhouse. I want my books. I want... I want the way it was.

I lean as close to Christopher's ear as I can and whisper, "I don't feel very good."

He quickly leans forward to the shelf of drinks and opens a can of soda. "Here, drink this. It's ginger ale and should help. Just close your eyes and take some deep breaths."

I take a sip and do exactly as he says, and I do start to feel better as the plane evens out.

"And now what?" Mrs. Davenport continues.

"Ember will be staying with me in New York. We have a lot to figure out and what the future has in store, but she'll be comfortable in my apartment and—"

"I sold your apartment and everything in it," Mrs. Davenport blurts. "I thought you were dead. You know how fast real estate goes in the city, and... I thought you were dead."

"Shit," Christopher says, leans his head against the headrest, and closes his eyes.

"I'm sorry."

"I understand. Like you said. You thought I was dead."

"It doesn't matter," Mrs. Davenport says in a cheerier voice than she has used before. "My townhouse has plenty of room for you. And considering all you've been through, I don't think you should be alone anyway. Your old room is still set up, and Ms. Evans will love having someone to cook for again, since I rarely seem to be home anymore with all the recent social engagements I've been busy with."

"*We*," Christopher says, looking at me with a reassuring smile, "would like that for now. At least until I find us a place to live."

Mrs. Davenport looks at me, back to Christopher, and then back at me. "Ember, do you not have any other family or friends? I'm sure they will be wanting to see you as soon as they can."

"No," I state softly. "My mother is dead, and Papa Rich... well... he was all I had."

A woman who stood by the door as we entered emerged from behind a curtain carrying a tray of sandwiches and bags of potato chips. "When you boarded, I know you said you were hungry. We don't have a lot on the plane," she begins, "but I do have these." She pulls out a table that comes from the shelf of drinks, and it serves as a centerpiece between Christopher and me and his mother. She places the food on the table, and Mrs. Davenport waves her away. She then walks away before any of us can say anything to her.

"So, you want Ember to stay with us?" Mrs. Davenport asks with a look on her face that seems as if she's tasted something bad.

"Mother," Christopher snaps. Then in a calmer voice, he adds, "I told you. She's my wife. So, yes, she'll be staying with me... with us."

"Well, she isn't exactly your wife. Not legally. I'm sure there was no marriage license, and even if there was, you were married under duress. This isn't legal or binding in the slightest. No one would blame you for thinking it wasn't. I'm sure Father Antonio wouldn't blame you one bit, and I seriously doubt we would even have to go forward with an annulment."

"Mom," Christopher says in a tone that rings of warning. "We can discuss this further later. But right now, my *wife* and I need to eat. We need to process. We need to not talk about what happened while we were there. I know you have a lot of questions, and I promise I will answer them soon. But for now, we need some peace. Please."

3

EMBER

Somehow, I manage to fall asleep using Christopher's shoulder as a pillow. I had tried to eat some, but my stomach and nerves wouldn't allow it. But sleep at least came, although it doesn't last for long.

I can hear Christopher and his mother talking as I go in and out of consciousness. He's telling her the story from the minute he was hit upside the head and shackled in the cellar, the deaths of the poor people trying to help us, our marriage, our escape... everything. I try to ignore the words and sleep. I don't want to hear what happened again. I don't want the images to flash in my mind, even though they seem to be forever seared in my memories.

"This is insane, Christopher," his mother says as I keep my eyes closed so they both think I'm asleep. "I understand why you feel responsible for this girl. I do. But you can't be expected to take care of her forever. You most certainly don't have to be married to her!" Her words are low, like a hiss from a snake.

"Shh!" Christopher snaps, and I feel his body tense beneath my cheek. "She might hear you."

"I don't care," his mother hisses again. "This isn't anything I wouldn't say to her face."

"I know you can't understand why I'm doing this. But Ember and I grew really close while we were trying to survive. I care for her, and in no way would I ever abandon her. So you need to get that out of your mind right now."

"She's going to have a lot of issues I don't think you're equipped to handle. What about your career? You are far from marriage material at this stage of your life."

"Yeah, she's got a lot of damage. But we both do. You don't think this experience fucked me up? Frankly, Ember is the only person who will ever truly understand me. That place changed me. Maybe for the worse, or maybe for the better. I can tell you I sure as fuck appreciate freedom and life right now."

"Jesus, what are people going to say? Everyone thought you were dead, when in fact you were kidnapped. But then you want us also to tell people you're married! Can you imagine the gossip this is going to cause? It's unreal!"

"Mom, lower your voice," Christopher whispers as he softly runs his hand over my head. "I don't want you to wake her. And I don't care what people say."

"Maybe you don't, but I do! And what about your job? Your reputation. You don't want to be a spectacle or thought of as some broken person."

"Maybe I am a bit broken. Have you considered that? And I understand Ember is too. Which is why we will stay together and figure this all out. I'm not going to leave her, and I'm not going to fight with you on this either. You need to trust that I'm doing what's right for me and what's right for her. I get it; I know we aren't married legally, but in my heart and in my mind, this girl is my wife. Something happened in Hallelujah Junction that will forever connect us and form a bond that can't be severed. So I need you to accept this. I need you to welcome Ember and make *her* feel accepted."

"I would never be rude to a guest. You know that."

"She's going to be more than just a guest, Mom, and you know it. I need you to be there for her. I need you to be there for the both of us."

I hear her release a heavy breath, but she says nothing more. The momentary silence allows me to fall back asleep. I dream of Hallelujah Junction. I see flames, I see Papa Rich, and I see the schoolhouse. Home. I see my home.

I wake up with a start when the wheels of the plane connect with the ground.

Christopher pats my lap in reassurance. "We're here safe and sound."

I blink away the sleep and notice Mrs. Davenport is staring at me once again. I try my best to not pay attention to the fact and instead run my fingers through my hair, wishing I had a brush.

"I arranged for a limo to pick us up," she says as she reaches for her purse and pulls out a small mirror and lipstick. She applies it with such skill and precision, and I'm once again envious.

"Shit!" Christopher says as he looks out the window.

I look over his shoulder and see cars and people all around the plane as it comes to a stop.

"The media," Mrs. Davenport says. She looks at Christopher and me and what we're wearing. "Oh my God."

"Someone at the police station must have tipped them off. Sold a story," Christopher says as he leans his head back against the chair, closing his eyes. "Paparazzi is not how I wanted to be welcomed home."

Mrs. Davenport pulls her mirror from her purse again and looks over her appearance once more. She then looks at me, reaches into her purse, and pulls out a small brush. "You may want to brush your hair, dear."

"Thank you," I say as I reach for the brush, grateful.

"Fuck. It's a goddamn madhouse out there," Christopher mumbles as he looks out the window again. "There's no avoiding them. I see the limo, but it's surrounded."

"I really wish you two were wearing something else," Mrs. Davenport says, shaking her head with disgust on her face. "I don't want these to be the first pictures people see."

Christopher turns to face me. "There's going to be a lot of flashing cameras, loud voices, and a million questions coming at us. I'm going to lead us through it as fast as I can, but just keep staring straight ahead, and don't say a thing. I've got this handled."

"What are you going to say?" Mrs. Davenport asks. "Should we prepare a speech before we get off the plane?"

Christopher shakes his head as he runs his fingers through his hair in frustration. "I'm not ready to give any kind of speech. I just want us to get to the limo as fast as we can. We'll deal with the media on another day. I'm sure this won't be the last we'll see of them."

"Why are they here?" I ask, my voice cracking from not using it for so long.

"Because of who we are," he answers. "My family's name keeps them interested in us."

"And because of what happened," Mrs. Davenport adds. "If they got wind of the story... this is going to be huge news." She reaches for her phone and starts hitting buttons. "I'm calling Jason. He'll help guide us through this."

"I can handle it," Christopher snaps as he unfastens his seatbelt and stands. I do the same, although my knees feel weak, and I worry I might fall.

"We pay Jason a lot of money to handle issues like this for us," she says, ignoring her son and his wishes completely.

I wait for him to get angry and demand respect as Papa Rich would do, but instead, Christopher leads me toward the exit of the plane. It appears his mother and he have an unknown language I'm not privy to.

He takes a deep breath as the woman who brought us the sandwiches waits for his signal on when to open the door. He looks at me one last time before we exit. "They're going to be taking our pictures. They are going to want to capture us and paint this story in the most glorified, horrific way. Don't give them any reason to make this worse than it is. Stare ahead. Keep your emotions at bay. Just focus on walking to the limo as fast as we can." He leans in and kisses me on the forehead. "It'll be over fast. I promise."

He seems afraid, and it doesn't take me long to know why. The minute we exit the plane, there is a wave of sound that nearly causes me to stumble down the steps. There are so many questions that all I hear is just a solid block of sound. Lights are flashing everywhere to where I nearly feel blind from them. I hear some questions, but they are all the same.

"Were you really chained in a basement for months?"

"Is this the famous Hallelujah Junction ghost? It's rumored your name is Ember. Is that true?"

"Were you really forced to marry the ghost while chained?"

"Were you held captive by the Hallelujah Junction serial killer?"

"How did you both escape? Is it true you burned the town to the ground?"

I try to look forward. I try not to show my fear. I try to do everything Christopher told me to do as he forces our way through bodies of people either shouting questions or taking our picture. I can't see the limo, but Christopher is tugging me along.

"Christopher, what's it like to come back from the dead?"

"Did they catch the serial killer? Is he still on the loose?"

I'm not sure where Mrs. Davenport is, but I assume she's close behind us, because I hear questions directed at her as well.

"Louisa, what's it like to have your son back after believing he was dead?"

"Is seeing your son like seeing a ghost?"

"What do you think about the ghost of Hallelujah Junction walking hand in hand with your son?"

I'm reminded of the desert thunderstorms of Hallelujah Junction. Ninety-mile-per-hour winds, lightning, thunder, and the smell of impending destruction. This is what I'm walking through.

Complete mayhem and chaos.

The purpose to break down our fragile walls as the weather would try to do to the old structures of the ghost town.

I can see the limo in the distance, and the driver is trying to make a path for us as we approach.

It's then that Christopher surprises me when he finally answers all the questions. "It's good to be home," he says with a smile and a wave.

It's the one and only thing spoken as we both duck into the limo, followed by a calm and composed

Mrs. Davenport. Both Christopher and his mother seem nearly relaxed, as if they hadn't just marched through a tornado. I, on the other hand, can barely breathe. The air of the limo seems thick and weighs heavy on my lungs.

"I left a message for Jason," his mother says as we begin to drive through the crowd of reporters. "He'll know what our next step needs to be."

"Our next step is getting home, getting showered, and trying to forget everything about Hallelujah Junction," he says as he leans his head back and closes his eyes.

He's not holding my hand anymore, and I realize I need it. I need it more than I've ever needed anything. Knowing I would earn another glare from his mother, I resist the urge to reach for it but instead clasp my fingers together in my lap.

I look out the window at the passing scenery and think about home. I think about Papa Rich and wonder if he's truly alive and hiding with Scarecrow. I think about when things were simpler, with my books and my cat, Pine Cone. I don't want to forget like Christopher does. If I forget, it will be as if I never existed. Hallelujah Junction might be Christopher's nightmare, but it's all I had. It's me.

I'm a walking nightmare Christopher brought along as a constant reminder.

Tears well in my eyes, but I blink them away.

How can I forget?

How can I move on?

What does moving on even look like?

So far, all I've seen are bright lights and shouting faces.

I'm nothing but the ghost of Hallelujah Junction stuck in a different kind of purgatory.

4

CHRISTOPHER

I'M NOT SURPRISED TO SEE MORE MEDIA WAITING outside the front of my mother's Upper East Side townhome. This circus isn't going away anytime soon, and I can't say I blame any of the reporters. Hell, if it weren't me being the object of fascination, I might be one of the photographers on the street myself in hopes of capturing the perfect picture for *Rolling Stone Magazine*. I understand their need to follow the story—it's a fucking unbelievable story—but I still hate seeing them flock around our shelter like vultures.

Luckily, the walk to the front door isn't far, and we can just usher right past them as fast as we can. An iron fence around the stoop is more welcomed now than ever before. It will offer us some protection from the masses.

I'm proud of Ember. I worried when we landed that seeing all the reporters all at once would cause her to have a panic attack of some sort and make a scene. I wouldn't have blamed her one bit, but instead, she remained steadfast and focused on just walking with her head held high and her shoulders back. Regardless how ridiculous we look in our hand-me-down outfits, the woman still appears stunning in my eyes. I am pretty sure there isn't a single picture that was captured that caught her in a bad light. She truly reminds me of an angel, and no doubt her essence will be seen by all who see these pictures.

"Ms. Evans is waiting for us. I told her to open the door the minute we approach," my mother says as she reads the texts on her phone. She hasn't looked away from the screen for even a second since getting in the limo. I am pretty sure every person she knows is texting her and wanting to get the scoop on her son being back from the dead before anyone else. In a sick way, I'm pretty sure my mother is loving every minute of it. Attention whore is a job description of a socialite.

"Ready?" I ask Ember. "Just like when we got off the plane. Just keep walking."

Her eyes dart to the reporters, then to me, and very slowly, she nods. "Ready."

The rush of blurred sound nearly drowns us. I've found myself on *Page Six* a time or two in my life, and I've been captured by the paparazzi a few times with my celebrity friends, but absolutely nothing could have prepared me for this insanity. It's louder and more aggressive than at the airport. Maybe because they know that once we are inside, we're safe and may never come back out. Regardless of how relentless they are in trying to get the best picture and to force me to answer their questions, we charge forward to the door that Ms. Evans now has opened for us.

When the three of us enter and the door is slammed behind us, it's as if we just escaped a blizzard and finally found shelter. I wrap an arm around Ember and kiss her on the forehead. I can't imagine how that had to feel for her, and yet she remained strong through it all.

"Christopher, it is so good to see you... alive!" Ms. Evans says as she stands before me, face pale, eyes wide, and mouth slightly ajar. "When your mother told me.... What a true blessing this is."

"Thank you, Ms. Evans. It's good to be home. Really good."

"Christopher?" I hear a shaky but familiar voice to my right.

I turn my head and see Marissa standing there. I realize she's been there all along, is watching me stand there with my arm around Ember, and is having to absorb the fact that her boyfriend she thought was dead is far from it. Out of respect for her, I take my arm off Ember and step away just to give a little more distance.

"Marissa," I say, but I have no idea what else to follow it with.

She closes the distance between us and hugs me. "When they told me you were dead...."

She starts sobbing against my shoulder, and I rub her back in comfort. I don't know what to do. I don't know what to say. I can feel Ember's eyes on me, but I don't have the courage to meet them.

"What happened?" she asks but doesn't pull her head away. "*How* did this happen?"

"A sick man knocked me out, kidnapped me, and made it look like I died. It's a long and twisted story I don't even know how to tell, to be honest."

"All that matters is that you're back," she mumbles against me, tightening her hold. "You've come back to me."

"Marissa," I say again, swallowing down the awkwardness I'm feeling, knowing I have to take this situation by the balls whether I want to or not. "I need to introduce you to someone." I break the embrace and take a few steps back so that I'm closer to Ember than I am to Marissa. "This is Ember. She was with me in Hallelujah Junction. We were held there together before we escaped."

Marissa looks at Ember and offers a weak smile as she wipes at the tears on her cheeks. "Ember, it's nice to meet you. I'm so happy Christopher didn't have to be alone while there."

"She's my wife," I blurt, not knowing how to say it gently and in a way not to hurt Marissa. I have to rip off the Band-Aid. She deserves to know the bitter truth as soon as possible.

Marissa takes a stumbling step back as if I just punched her in the face. She scans Ember from head to toe and then looks at me. "Your wife? What are you talking about?"

"The man—Richard—who held me captive forced me to marry Ember. He considered Ember his daughter and... well, I was kidnapped with the intention for me to marry his daughter."

"Christopher was *forced* to marry her," my mother chimes in. "He had no choice. He was chained to a wall, and after that, he was chained to this girl."

I still can't look at Ember. I should. I should stand by her side and hold her hand in solidarity, but at the same time, the pain that is now on Marissa's face is killing a piece of me slowly. I don't want to hurt her. Hell... I don't want to hurt anyone. But there is no way I can walk away from this situation without someone's heart getting decimated.

"You're married now?" Marissa asks in disbelief. "Why would you...? Married?

"Not really. Not legally," my mother tries to reassure as she looks at Ember with a level of disgust on her face I've never seen before. "He was kidnapped. He had to do what he had to do to survive."

I finally look at Ember, who is staring at Marissa with just as much confusion and shock as Marissa has painted on her face.

"What about us?" Marissa asks. "What about *me*?"

"I know this is hard," I begin, trying to find the right words. But what the fuck can I say? In Marissa's eyes, I died, I came back to life, and now I'm married. All without a formal breakup or closure.

Do I break up with her?

Isn't the situation obvious?

I run my fingers through my hair as my head spins. What is the fucking situation? I don't even know it myself.

Ms. Evans tries to cut through the awkward air. "Can I get anyone anything to eat or drink?" I don't blame the woman one bit for wanting to flee to the kitchen.

"No, thank you. I think Ember and I need to go get showered and some rest," I say, knowing I too want to flee this room, but I understand I can't just run from my problems. "Marissa... I understand this is a lot to take in. I wish I had all the right things to say, but I don't know what they are. All I know is that right now, I have to take things one minute at a time. I need to shower. I need to process. I need to breathe. I also understand that you have questions. Lots of questions. But can we discuss this all tomorrow? It's been a really long day after months of even longer days. Can you give me that?" I look to my mother. "Can you both give me that?"

"I've prepared your old room for you, Christopher, and I also prepared the guest room for Ember," Ms. Evans says.

"No need for the guest room. We'll both be using mine," I inform everyone.

"Christopher!" my mother says with a loud gasp as she takes a step toward Marissa in a sign of camaraderie and loyalty. "I think that's far from appropriate. I think Ember will be perfectly comfortable in the guest room."

"I'm not going to leave Ember alone right now. I made a promise, and I'm going to stick to it."

I know I'm hurting Marissa. I know I'm upsetting my mother. But as I take Ember's hand to lead her upstairs, I also know I have a responsibility to Ember... to my wife.

"Christopher," my mother calls to me as we are at the top of the stairs. I prepare to spin on my heels and snap her head off. I'm losing patience, and I am in no mood to have her argue with me as to where Ember's going to sleep. "I'll give some of my clothes to Ember until we have a chance to go shopping. We look like we are close in size. I also had some of your old belongings boxed up. Ms. Evans pulled the clothes out for you."

Surprised by her act of kindness to a woman who I can clearly see she dislikes, I look over my shoulder and give her a smile. "Thank you, Mom. I appreciate that." I glance at Marissa, who has tears in her eyes and a blotchy face. "We can all meet and talk it out tomorrow. Goodnight."

When we enter my room, I release a deep breath I didn't realize I must have been holding. It's odd to see my old room, not that it really was my room from my childhood. My mother completely remodeled it when I went off to college, so it's really just another guest room with a queen-sized bed, dressers, and nightstands imported from Paris. She was so proud of the room, but it wasn't my taste at all. I much preferred clean, modern lines over the antique feel, but it made my mother happy.

When I close the door, Ember speaks for the first time. "Who is Marissa?"

Jesus, I need sleep and don't feel like talking anymore, but I also know Ember deserves her questions answered. "She was my girlfriend before."

"Why didn't you tell me?"

"There's a lot about me and my life prior to meeting you that you don't know, Ember. You have to understand that. But should I have told you I had a girlfriend? Yes. And I apologize. I should have prepared you for this—although, in all fairness, I didn't think she'd be waiting for me the minute I arrived home. I thought I'd have some time."

"You had a girlfriend? But you married me?" she asks softly, and although I'm growing frustrated with the situation—it's not like any of this is my fucking fault—I try to keep my calm. Ember doesn't deserve my wrath.

"I didn't have a choice in marrying you." The minute the words leave my mouth, I regret them.

Ember nearly wobbles to the edge of the bed and sits down, looking down at the oriental rug. She kicks off her shoes and wiggles her freed toes.

"I understand that," Ember says as she then looks up at me. "But we're married now. I know your mother says we aren't. But I believe we are. Under God, we are. In my heart and soul, we are. How do you feel?"

Her blue eyes so full of truth stab me in the heart. She's calm, she's collected, and she seems so wise and in control. In a whirlwind of chaos, standing in this room with Ember is the first time I feel a sense of grounding.

"You're my wife," I say. "I don't care what anyone says; you *are* my wife."

"And Marissa?"

"I will need to handle the situation delicately. I don't want to hurt her. I don't want to hurt you. But I can't think right now. I'm tired. I need a shower. *We* need a shower. Tomorrow is another day, and we can face this nightmare then." I point to the closed door. "You can have the shower first. I'll go see about some of my mother's clothes while you're in there."

Ember stands up and walks to me. Inches from my face, she tilts her head up so she can look directly into my eyes. "I'm sorry, Christopher. I'm sorry you have to go through all this. You don't deserve this."

I run my hand down the back of her head and pull her into an embrace. "You have nothing to apologize for. I'm sorry for both of us. This situation is so fucked up."

"Do you regret taking me with you?" she mumbles against me.

"Never," I say, pulling her away enough so that I can kiss her lips. The act of intimacy feels foreign, as if I shouldn't be kissing my wife. "Yes, we made wedding vows, but I made my own vow to you that has nothing to do with being married. I'm never going to leave you, Ember. I'm here for you through all of this." I kiss her one more time, determined for the sensation to not feel wrong, but it still seems off in the light of normalcy and no longer being chained together. "I'm not going to lie to you and tell you this is going to be easy. It's not. It's going to be fucking hard. Really fucking hard."

"But we'll get through it," she finishes for me. "Together."

God, I fucking hope so. I do.

"Christopher?"

"Tomorrow," I interrupt, having reached my max. "Tomorrow."

"But—"

"Ember... I need to... tomorrow."

I know the tone in my voice is harsh. I know I should hold her. I should make promises and reassurances to her. I should put her feelings first.

But right now, all I can do is shut down. My mind says enough. My heart splinters with every sign of my past life muddling my current. The situation is swallowing me up, and I worry I can't be who I need to be and do what I need to do.

Bells are ringing in my ears. Flashes of insanity are approaching.

"Tomorrow," Ember finally says, her voice pulling me from the depths.

5

EMBER

IT SMELLS DIFFERENT.

It sounds different.

It feels different.

This isn't my home. This isn't Hallelujah Junction.

And though I'm lying in bed next to Christopher, I don't recognize anything. Not even him. The man last night was different than I've ever seen. *Everything* is different.

The borrowed nightgown I wear feels too soft—like butter. It slides on my skin, and I feel molested by cloth that's not mine. The sheets feel that way as well. Rich and luxurious but suffocating.

I don't belong here, but regardless, I am here. Where else can I go? Even if I wanted to go back to Hallelujah Junction, it is burned to the ground by my own doing.

"Did you sleep well?" Christopher asks huskily as he rolls over to face me. His eyes sparkle in the sunlight peeking through the curtains.

"No." I don't want to lie to Christopher. I'm not a liar... yet. Maybe this place will change me.

He stretches and yawns. "I know this is a lot to get used to. It'll take time."

With a small groan, Christopher gets out of bed and pads barefoot over to the window, opening the curtain. He's wearing nothing but underwear, and I'm surprised when a stirring in my sex ignites at the sight. I try to divert my sinful eyes, but I can't. He looks down below and curses. "Shit. They're still here."

"The reporters? Why?" How can we be so interesting that people choose to camp outside?

"They know we have to come out someday. They are hunters waiting for their prey.

"I'm scared," I confess.

He looks over his shoulder at me and offers a warm smile. "You don't need to be scared. They seem scary, but they're harmless. Remember, I'm a photographer myself... or I was."

"Not of them," I clarify. "But what if... if we're on television or the newspapers, then *he* can find us. Papa Rich. If he's alive, he'll know where we are."

I sit up, feeling as if I have to in order for the thick mattress not to swallow me up.

"That's not possible."

"How can you be so sure? I know Papa Rich. And if he's alive, he'll want me back with him. He'll want us both. He won't give up until that happens. He's always claimed to be a determined and driven man. He says God gave him the gift of fortitude."

Christopher takes two large strides toward me with a firm jaw and narrowed eyes. His voice is low and terse. "Don't ever be afraid of that man again. You hear me? He's had enough control over our lives for a lifetime. I will not allow him to control another minute any longer." He sits down next to me on the bed and takes my hand in his. His voice softens as he adds, "I'm never going to let you be in danger again. If he's alive... *if*... he better stay away. Because I won't hesitate to kill him myself. He's never getting you again. You aren't his to take. You're mine now."

"Am I yours?" I ask, liking the way it sounds but not truly believing him.

"Yes, mine."

"It doesn't feel that way," I admit. "Your mother is right. You were forced to marry me. She doesn't see me as your wife. No one will." I look out the window and see the blue in the sky. "I'm not even sure you see me as your wife."

"It doesn't matter what others think," he says, rubbing a circle on my hand with his fingertip. "It's about what you and I feel. And right now, I feel more connected to you than I do anything else. My life feels out of control right now. But you are my one grounding constant. You are the one person who truly understands what I went through and what I'm feeling now. I don't care about the term 'wife' or all the legalities. We're together. I'm not leaving you, and that's all that matters." He brushes a lock of hair behind my ear. "You're my wife, Ember. Block out all the noise that says anything different."

He leans forward and places his lips to mine. It's not like last night's kisses. It's different. I hear his breath. I feel his breath. And when he pushes his tongue into my mouth, I taste his breath. It's laced with hunger and need that matches my own.

He pulls away just enough to whisper, "I'm not letting you go. I know you're afraid I will, but I swear to you, you're mine. My wife. My future."

The kiss continues and deepens even more as he lowers me back down to the mattress, mounting me as he does so. Effortlessly, he pulls down his underwear, and it dawns on me that this is the first time we have been able to do this action without a chain to our ankles. We're free... at least from the metal constraints.

Christopher doesn't waste any time removing my clothes fully but instead pushes my nightgown up over my breasts. I'm not wearing any panties, so there is nothing getting in the way of his sex and mine. He nudges my thighs wider, making room for him as he lowers his mouth to my neck and nibbles a trail of lust.

With one hard push, he enters inside, spreading me wide with his thickness. I inhale deeply as my pussy adjusts to his size. He pauses for a moment as he's rooted deep within.

I welcome the connection even more than the feeling. I *need* him in me. I need to feel us as one when I feel he's slipping away. I groan when he pulls out of me, but then I cry out when he thrusts back in. The slickness of my desire makes it easy for him to push and pull at a speed that brings me to climax faster than I had ever been able to before. It's easier this time. I'm not worried about pleasing him and being a good wife in the schoolhouse as the smell of ghosts and secrets surrounds us.

Right now, it's just about having the man I love deep inside me and never wanting him out. We're safe here. We're one. No one can hurt me, or him, or *us*.

The feeling of fear is replaced with a feeling of passion and sensuality. I move my body with his as his moans intensify. His nibbles turn into a bite, and then another. But I like the pain. I like the sting as it reminds me of where I am. It grounds me and puts me beneath the weight of Christopher.

"Harder," I whisper.

A growl emerges from deep inside him, and he hikes my leg up on his hip and drives himself into me farther. He's so deep it feels as if he's nearly bruising my body where only he can touch. The discomfort is almost punishing but also primal in my need for more. I want the discipline of his cock to remind my body and soul that he will never leave me. He will never release his duties of husband and protector. I need his dick to beat the reminder inside me. Over and over. Harder and harder, I need it. *I need it!*

This is *my* Christopher. *My* husband.

He's having sex with *me*. He's claiming *me*.

Me.

Not Marissa.

Not anyone else.

Me.

His wife.

Christopher thrusts even deeper and harder now as if he can feel my hunger for the biting erotic pain. He palms my breast now as he drives forward, with a deep moan following. I feel a second wave of electricity building inside as he pinches my nipple. His eyes connect with mine, and I like that I can see them darken and nearly blur. He's present but also far away. I can feel his own climax is nearing, and as I jerk my hips up to meet him thrust for thrust, his deep roar blends with my own moans of completion.

The weight of his body is on top of me now, and his rapid breathing is slowing as it matches cadence with mine.

"I don't ever want you to doubt me," he whispers against my hair. "I'm committed to you. I'm committed to us."

I cling to his ass with my fingers, holding him inside me. I don't want his dick to leave my pussy. I like it there. I want it to remain always, but I also know we can't hide in this bed forever.

"What happens today?" I ask, truly having no idea what life is like now that we are free from the ghost town.

Rolling over, Christopher stares up at the ceiling for several moments. "I don't know. I really don't. I have to somehow figure out how to get my life back. My job, a place for us to live. I also need to figure out a statement to give the media. They won't go away until I deal with it." He turns his head and looks at me. "What do *you* want to happen?"

I don't know the answer.

I shrug. "I don't know. I try to picture tomorrow, and it's blank. I can't see what's ahead of us."

"I get that," he says, looking sad for a brief moment. "But we'll figure it out."

"How do I get your mother to like me?" I ask. I might be naive in a lot of ways. I know that. But I'm not so naive to know that his mother doesn't like me one bit, and I want to change that.

He sighs loudly. "Give her time. This is a lot for her to process too. This isn't how she wanted it for me. My mother would have thrown a huge wedding that would have been the party of the year. There would have been engagement parties, rehearsal dinners, and basically anything that would mean her planning a special event. She loves that kind of stuff."

"Was she going to do that for you and Marissa?" I ask, leaning up on my elbow so I can look at Christopher better.

"Marissa and I were not discussing marriage or anywhere near that level. We were dating, having a good time, but very casual." He pauses. "For me at least. I'm sure she would have liked to be more serious, but I was far from marriage material. My life wasn't conducive to being a husband."

"But you're a husband now."

He closes his eyes briefly and then looks at me with a seriousness I'm not familiar with seeing on him. "I am now, which means I have to figure out a life where it's conducive."

"I wish you would have told me about her," I admit. I wanted to tell him this last night, but he cut our night short, which I didn't blame him for.

"Would it have made a difference?" he asks softly.

Feeling a twinge of shame, I shake my head. "I suppose not." Papa Rich had planned for us to be married no matter what. And if Christopher refused, Papa Rich would have killed him. I know this. Christopher knows this.

"My mother is not an easy woman," he says as he sits up and reaches for his underwear. "Deep down, she means well. I know she loves me. But she's not easy." He looks at me and nods at my disheveled nightgown. "I'm surprised she gave you that. She also gave you a dress to wear to breakfast. As soon as we can figure out what's in store for us today, we'll get you some clothes, shoes, undergarments, et cetera, for you of your own." He leans down on the bed with his hands and gives me a kiss. "I'm new at all this stuff. So, I'm going to need you to tell me what you want or don't want. I need your input, okay?"

I nod and smile, happy I recognize Christopher again. "Okay."

"We better get downstairs. I'm sure they're waiting for us with a million questions."

"I'll make us breakfast," I offer. "I don't know what's in the pantry, but I'm pretty good at making do. Is there anything your mother doesn't like to eat?"

Christopher chuckles. "Cooking is not a good idea. Not if you want to keep your hands. Ms. Evans will hack them off if you dare."

"She makes the meals?" I've never eaten anything that I haven't made myself. I've always done all the cooking.

"She cooks and cleans for my mother. She has for years. She's like family around here."

"Can I help?" I don't like the idea of having some other woman do all the work. I had read about servants in books, but is Ms. Evans a servant? Shouldn't we all pitch in to help?

"For right now, I think you need to just focus on getting settled in to this new way of life. You and I are going to be busy figuring everything out. Let Ms. Evans worry about the basics."

I must have a look on my face revealing just how uncomfortable I am with the idea of not earning my keep.

"Don't worry," he adds. "When you and I have our own place again, you can make all your famous recipes that I grew to love." He reaches over and pats my leg. "Come on. Get dressed. I'm hungry, and I can hear the thoughts of my mother now. She's pacing the floor. I can bet anything on that right now."

Not an easy woman, Christopher says.

Not an easy woman.

I guess Papa Rich wasn't an easy man.

I've had practice.

6

EMBER

IT'S LOUD WHEN WE WALK DOWNSTAIRS. I HEAR voices, and the first thing I see is the television on with both Christopher and me on the screen. I'm on television. My face is on television.

Christopher walks straight to the TV and stands in front of it. I stay near him, because I feel I need to in order to be defended against the storm about to hit, but I divert my eyes from the screen. I don't want to see it. I don't want to stare the devil that was our past straight in the eye.

"Fuck," Christopher says under his breath.

"Oh good, you two are finally up," Mrs. Davenport says as she enters the room followed by a man in a suit and tie, his hair slicked back, and black glasses that seem to barely balance on the edge of his nose. "Jason and I've been waiting. He's come up with some good ideas for us to get ahead of this situation."

"Looks like the situation is already moving along full force without us," Christopher says, still watching the news on the television.

"As I was telling Louisa," Jason says, "I've started to work on a statement for you to say. Right now, the media sees you both as victims, which means they are going to be sympathetic to your need for privacy during this difficult time. At least on the surface. Everyone will want to get the full scoop, so we need to decide who we're giving the story to."

Christopher turns away from the television and sighs. He then places a hand on my lower back and starts to lead me out of the room. "At least allow Ember and me to get some breakfast in us before we start planning for battle."

Louisa chimes in, "We need to listen to Jason. He knows how to handle—"

"I get it, Mom," Christopher snaps, and I suddenly see the man from last night that I don't recognize. I instantly want the man I was just in bed with to return.

The phone rings as we both take our seats at a long wooden table. An elegant chandelier hangs above us, and the glass is reflecting beams of light around the room. I don't feel comfortable. I don't want to touch the table in fear of leaving fingerprints on the shiny surface.

Ms. Evans pokes her head out from a door. "Oh good, you are both here. I'll have your breakfast out in a second. I hope you're hungry."

I start to get up to help her, but Christopher places his hand on my lap to signal for me to sit. Remembering the conversation from earlier about Ms. Evans not wanting help in the kitchen, I remain in place and... wait. I've never had someone bring me food before when all I do is sit at a table. I don't like it. I like to feel useful. I like to serve the ones I love. I want to be Christopher's wife and cook him a breakfast I know he'll love. Ms. Evans isn't his wife; I am. What would Papa Rich say if he knew I'm just sitting here doing nothing?

"Christopher," Mrs. Davenport says from the threshold of the doorway. "The phone's for you. It's your editor at *Rolling Stone.*"

"I'll be right back," Christopher says to me as he gets up from the chair, takes the phone from his mother, then walks to the other room.

Mrs. Davenport then redirects her attention to me, walks up to the table, and stares down at my bare feet.

"We wear shoes at the dining table in this house," she says between clenched teeth and low enough in tone that only I can hear her.

I glance down at my toes and then back at her, embarrassed I've clearly displeased her. "I'm sorry. I don't know what happened to the slippers the police gave us. When I got out of the shower last night, everything was gone."

"Christopher had everything thrown away. I can't say I blame him. He'll want to forget every part of his horrible ordeal, and I'll do my best to make sure he can."

So, if she knows my shoes were thrown away, why would she question that I don't have any shoes on?

Ms. Evans enters the dining room with two plates of breakfast. "I wasn't sure how you took your eggs, so I made omelets just to be safe for today."

"What size shoe do you wear?" Mrs. Davenport asks, still towering over me.

"I don't know."

"What do you mean, you don't know?"

"I didn't wear shoes before."

Her mouth opens wide, her eyes even wider. "What do you mean? You never wore a pair of shoes in your life?"

I steal a glance at Ms. Evans, who just stands motionless with the plates in her hands. I then look at Mrs. Davenport, resentful that I have to discuss this memory that I'd rather not. "Papa Rich didn't allow me to wear shoes."

"You poor girl," Ms. Evans says softly as she places the plates of food in front of me and Christopher's chair.

Mrs. Davenport clutches her neck for a moment and then gently massages the skin. "Well... Ms. Evans, can you go upstairs and try to find a pair of shoes that might fit her of mine. Her foot doesn't look too different than my own." She looks at the dress I'm wearing. "My dress seems to fit you fine enough."

I nod, looking at the pale pink dress, and force a smile. "Thank you. It fits perfectly."

When I got dressed this morning in the dress and walked out of the bathroom to Christopher, his nose wrinkled, and he told me that we would need to get me my own clothes immediately. He obviously didn't like seeing me in his mother's clothing. I wonder what he will think seeing me wear her shoes.

"I think you should follow Ms. Evans upstairs to receive the shoes," she continues. When I look at my breakfast, she says, "Your meal will still be here when you return. Plus, it would be rude to eat before Christopher returns to the table."

Her tone of voice reminds me of Papa Rich's when he feels I don't do something Godly. I know better than to ever question that tone.

Without saying another word, I scoot my chair out, stand up, and follow Ms. Evans up the stairs barefoot. I can almost feel Mrs. Davenport's stare singeing the flesh on my back.

Mrs. Davenport's foot is a little bigger than mine, but not by much. Ms. Evans finds a pair that she feels will do. "This pair is a bit smaller," she says. "Mrs. Davenport will suffer for style and squeeze her feet into shoes that are a bit too small if she has to. Lucky for you."

I reach for the black heels and wonder if they will be considered too fancy, but I also know I don't have a choice. And looking around Mrs. Davenport's closet—which is as large as a bedroom

—I don't see any simple shoes or boots. Everything seems so... expensive and luxurious.

"I'm sorry I didn't help with breakfast," I say, feeling the need to apologize regardless of what Christopher said. The woman seems so kind, and I want her to know how I feel.

"Sorry? Why would you say such a thing? There's nothing to be sorry about."

"I did all the cooking before. Before...."

The smile and cheery disposition she had seem to melt off her face. A sadness appears to wash over her. "I understand how all this has to be really scary and different. It's a completely different world you're now in."

Tears prickle the backs of my eyes, but I refuse to allow them to surface.

"I can't imagine what you and Christopher went through." She waits for me to place the shoes on my feet and then helps me find my balance as I wobble on the heels. "Is what they're saying on the news true? Where you kidnapped as a child and forced to live hidden in a schoolhouse, never to see another soul?"

I take a cautious step and then another. "I never saw it that way growing up." I take another step and worry I may twist my ankle if I'm not careful. "Papa Rich was my family."

"He sounds like a very sick and demented man."

I wonder what the news is saying about him. What are they saying about me?

"I don't know," I say. "I don't know."

"Were you happy there?"

"No," I admit. "No, I wasn't happy. But then I met Christopher."

The woman doesn't say anything for several awkward moments but then finally breaks the thick air by saying, "Well, let's head downstairs. Your breakfast is getting cold."

Making my way downstairs is no easy task. Shoes are hard enough to get used to, but heels are a different beast within themselves. They hurt my feet, make my ankles tired, and my calves seem to be tense at all times. I somehow get to the dining room without falling at the same time Christopher is getting off the phone and taking his own seat at the shiny table.

"Is everything okay?" he asks me with a look of confusion as to why I was gone.

"We just got her a pair of Mrs. Davenport's shoes to wear," Ms. Evans says with a warm smile.

Christopher glances down at my feet and then at his mother, who is now sitting at the head of the table, sipping from a teacup.

"Really, Mother? You can't give her a little grace? Heels?"

Mrs. Davenport raises an eyebrow and then places her teacup on the matching saucer below. "A lady only wears heels."

I take my seat and place my hand on Christopher's lap as he did with me when I tried to stand up to help. "Thank you, Mrs. Davenport. I appreciate you lending me the shoes."

"You can call her Louisa," Christopher says as he takes a bite of omelet. "No need for formalities."

"Well, we don't exactly know each other," Mrs. Davenport cuts in.

"She'll be calling you *Louisa*," Christopher says with a warning voice.

His mother must know when to not push any further when it comes to her son, because even though her lips purse together and wrinkles furrow her brow, she nods curtly and says, "Very well. Yes, please call me Louisa, dear."

I don't know this woman one bit, but I do know she doesn't mean a single word she says. But I also know it's Christopher's wishes, and I'll do as he asks just as his mother will.

"What did your work have to say?" she asks while she watches Christopher and me eat.

"They want me back," Christopher says between mouthfuls. "Jason is on the phone with them now about giving them an exclusive with me and Ember. We need to give it to someone, so why not *Rolling Stone*? He's working out all the details."

"That's excellent news," Louisa says. "It will do you good to get your old life back as soon as possible."

"We're going to start looking for an apartment as soon as possible too," he adds.

"Do you really think that's a good idea?" she asks. "With everything going on, and with the media circus, you may be better off staying here." She looks at me and then paints a smile on her face that makes the corners twitch. I'm learning this smile. I see the fake laced in it. "Think of Ember. If you go back to work with *Rolling Stone*, it will mean Ember being left alone. At least by you two staying here for a bit, she'll never be alone. Ms. Evans will be here."

I notice she doesn't say *she* will be here for me, but instead the servant doing the job of a wife and now the new caretaker. I don't want to be alone at all, but I also don't feel welcomed here regardless of what Louisa is saying.

"You have a point," he says as he takes large swallows of his orange juice. I notice it's not freshly squeezed. I would have squeezed it myself this morning before pouring him a glass.

Jason enters the room and pauses until all eyes are on him. "I have a statement written up for you," he says. "I think it's best for you to do it now. I also spoke with *Rolling Stone*, and all the details are ironed out for you."

Christopher wipes his mouth and stands. "Thank you, Jason, but I can handle the statement myself."

He then looks at me. "Are you done with breakfast? You barely touched your food."

My stomach churns with nerves, and I worry about keeping down the little food I did eat. "I'm done. I'm just nervous."

Christopher helps me out of the chair and says, "Let's get this over with. Just stand by my side, and I'll handle the rest." He takes my hand in his and walks us to the front door. "Remember, it's going to be loud, aggressive, and there will be a lot of flashing lights. Just do what you did yesterday. I saw us on television, and you looked great. You're really photogenic and controlled your emotions perfectly."

Christopher's praise doesn't make me feel any better, but I give him a weak smile. "I'm ready."

When the front door opens, the roar of chaos returns. I can't make out individuals in the crowd, because the flashing lights are so intense. I stay by Christopher's side as he lifts his arm to signal to the horde that he's about to say something.

"I'm happy to be home," he begins. "As you can imagine, this is a lot for me and my family to process. The ordeal I went through was not an easy one or one I wish for anyone to experience. What I witnessed and endured by the hands of a mad man is frankly, unbelievable. But we are home now, and we're safe." He looks at me. "While in captivity, I met this wonderful and courageous woman standing next to me. Although I was living a nightmare, Ember became my one light that got me through it all. Yes, she is what you are all calling the ghost of Hallelujah Junction, but she is made of flesh and bone and feelings. So please take that into consideration with your reporting. The two of us have a lot to adjust to with our new freedom, but we know that with time and understanding from all, we will recover and move on. I ask for our privacy as we take things one day at a time."

"Christopher!"

"Christopher!"

"Christopher!"

So many questions are shooting out at rapid speed. I can't make out any of them and wonder if Christopher can. I hear my name, I hear his name, and I hear Richard being called out. But what the sentences are exactly, I can't tell.

"Ember and I will be answering all your questions soon enough. For now, I ask for our privacy. Thank you."

Jason walks in front of us and calls out, "The family will be issuing a formal statement later today. But right now, Christopher and Ember need time to heal and recover."

He then tightens his grip on mine and turns us around to enter the house once again.

Safe.

But I feel anything but.

7

CHRISTOPHER

"I HAVE A SURPRISE," I TELL EMBER AFTER A LONG day fielding phone calls.

The FBI had been relentless, asking to speak to both Ember and me several times throughout the day. They kept asking the same questions over and over, and it was enough that I finally decided to hire an attorney. Although no one had gone straight out and said as much, I got the feeling they were questioning whether Ember was an accomplice in the murders Richard committed. I need to make sure they don't paint that picture or somehow trap Ember into saying something that could hurt her.

Jason—which then means my mother as well—doesn't like the optics of us hiring legal counsel, but I have to put my wife first. They keep saying that *I* didn't do anything wrong. And that *I* was a victim. But not once do they say *we*—including Ember. And if they didn't necessarily feel Ember is innocent, then who knows what the authorities and even a judge and jury will believe. It's time to lawyer up. No doubt about it.

Ember lifts her eyes to me, the blue nearly being swallowed up by the dark circles underneath. Her knees are pulled up to her chest, and she rests her head on them. She hasn't said much unless she has to answer direct questions. And though I feel like I've really gotten to know a lot about her with all our constant time held captive together, there is still so much I don't know. I wish I could read her better. I wish I could hear her thoughts.

"Surprise?"

"Come on. I just got off the phone with a really good friend of mine who is doing us a favor. It means we're going to have to make a run for the car I just ordered, but once we do, it's going to be fun from then on."

My mother is standing by the couch, nervously spinning the diamond rings on her fingers. "You aren't really going somewhere, are you? With all those reporters out there? It's not safe,

Christopher. Security isn't arriving until tomorrow morning."

"We won't need security. Don't worry. I got this handled. I'm taking Ember shopping."

"Shopping!" she spits out with shock. "You can't be serious."

"I am. I just got off the phone with Christina, and she's shutting down her boutique for us. We're going to come in from the back alley. Even if we're followed or seen, her doors will be locked while we shop." I look at Ember and smile. "We'll have the entire place to ourselves."

Rather than being afraid as I had expected from Ember, she instead seems curious and even happy to have a chance to get out of the house. I can't blame her. It does feel as if the walls are closing in on us.

Watching the town car pull up to the front, I reach for Ember's hand and help her up off the couch. I don't wait for my mother to object or for Jason to tell me that I'm about to create a PR nightmare. This isn't about anyone but me and Ember.

We need to breathe.

We need to be free.

We need to have a moment where we aren't trapped in the house just like we were trapped in Hallelujah Junction.

As we walk to the front door, I can hear my mother mumbling under her breath, but it's quickly replaced by the roar of the reporters and photographers as we bolt toward the awaiting car.

Once we are safe and driving off, Ember speaks for the first time. "Are you sure we'll be safe?"

"I'm sure." I pat her leg reassuringly and add, "Besides, you can't wear my mother's clothing and her ridiculous heels for long. And I need new stuff as well. It's time we get our lives started."

"I've never been shopping before," she says as she stares out the window at all the scenery passing by.

I can't imagine what it all must be like for her. To see such tall buildings and bright lights. Everything is new for her. Unknown. To do something as simple as shopping for the first time at twenty-five years of age... it's still unbelievable to me.

Every time I find myself about to completely lose my shit—which is often since arriving home—I pause and remind myself that no matter how bad I have it, Ember has it worse. When I want to punch my fist through a wall, or scream out in frustration, or tell everyone around me to go fuck themselves... I look at Ember. Just like in the schoolhouse of a rundown ghost town, she is still my beacon of light. She is still what keeps me sane. She is still my grounding force in all this madness. The least I can do is try to keep my cool and return the favor by at least appearing strong for her.

"My friend Christina has an excellent clothing store. We'll be able to get whatever you want there, and she's anxious to meet you. She said she's already pulling out items she thinks you'll love."

I have to hand it to the driver; he somehow manages to quickly take side streets and loses all the media. I know it's only momentary until they somehow track us down, as they have a scent for a good story like a hound dog for a hunt, but for right now, we have peace. Ember and I are both able to walk into the back door of Christina's without anyone there snapping a picture or asking a million questions. I'm happy to see my friend covered the front glass windows so no one will be able to see us from the front.

"You were able to lose them," she says with a smile as she ushers us in the door.

"Not sure for how long," I reply.

She gives me a long, hard hug, then pulls away to make eye contact that tells me all I need to know. She's happy I'm alive and well. She doesn't say anything, which I'm happy for. I need a break, and oddly... Christina seems to know it.

When we make our way to the main part of the store, she gives the warmest smile to Ember and extends her hand. "You must be Ember. I'm Christina. I've heard a lot about you."

Ember reaches out and shakes her hand, and I'm happy to see her return the smile right back. I haven't seen Ember really smile since the escape— at least not a genuine one.

"It's really nice of you to open your store for us," she says as she glances around at the rows and rows of clothing that flank the walls.

"Christopher is an old and dear friend. There isn't anything I wouldn't do for him." She turns to me and says, "Michael is also shutting his restaurant down an hour early tonight so we can go have dinner without curious eyes."

"You don't have to do that," I say, shaking my head. "You've already done enough for us by allowing us to shop in privacy."

Christina waves her hand and rolls her eyes. "It's done. Don't even try to argue. You're both having dinner with us, and that's it. Michael would kill me if I didn't make it happen. Once we max out your credit card, the least I can do is have my husband cook you both a great meal." She winks at me before looking Ember over from head to toe. "I think I have some great options for you that are going to fit absolutely perfect." She places her arm around Ember's shoulders and leads her to a rack of dresses. "Let's go break Christopher's bank."

Ember glances over her shoulder at me for reassurance that all is fine, but her smile is still present and even brighter than before. I nod and then turn to the side of the store that carries the men's clothing. "You ladies do all the damage you want. Ember has an empty closet that needs to be filled."

I appreciate that Christina doesn't treat either of us like a pity case. She doesn't ask us questions, even though I know she's dying to. I also love that she is being so welcoming and kind to Ember. She's the first person to truly do so since we escaped, unless you count Ms. Evans, but even Ms. Evans stared at us as if we were walking ghosts. Not Christina. She sees me as her friend, and she sees Ember as the woman I love.

"She needs undergarments, shoes... everything," I say as I start searching for my size in a pile of nicely folded jeans. I then steal a look at Christina, who is holding a dress up to Ember. "I think Ember will prefer flats too. My mother is trying to break her ankles in those heels she loaned her."

Rather than brushing me off or telling me that women must wear what's in style, Christina nods and says, "I have the cutest ballet flats that are going to look amazing on you. We have several colors, and I think Christopher's credit card demands to have one of each."

I laugh, watch Ember hold back laughter with mischief in her eyes that I love seeing, and call out, "Whatever Ember wants."

What feels like an eternity of watching Ember go into the changing room, out of the changing room in clothes that fit her perfectly, and then back into the changing room to repeat, and repeat, and repeat, we are finally done. I don't even look at the final total, nor do I care. I would buy the entire store for Ember if she wanted it. The woman deserves to be pampered, even though she doesn't even know what that is.

"Is there anything left in the store?" I tease, but I walk up to Ember, wrap my arms around her from behind, and kiss the side of her neck. "You looked beautiful in everything."

"Oh, I had a little mercy," Christina says. "A little."

"Are you sure?" Ember asks as she looks at me for approval. "We don't have to get everything if you feel it's too much."

"Let's bring the bags to the driver," I say, ignoring her concern. "He can bring them home while we're having dinner." I give Ember a kiss on her forehead. "It's the first of many shopping trips. You'll never do without or have to borrow clothing from anyone again."

I spin her around to get one more look at her, which has her blushing and laughing lightly. Ember remains in a dress from the shop that has flowers on it. It sort of reminds me of the floral dresses she wore in Hallelujah Junction, but it actually fits her, isn't faded, and is modern and from this decade.

I look down at her feet in a pair of beige flats and ask, "Do those feel all right?"

She follows my gaze to her feet and says, "They still feel... restrictive. But much better than those other awful shoes I was wearing. How do women wear those all day?"

"We're masochists, my friend. Masochists," Christina says with a sparkling laugh. "But no need to be like us. You look amazing today, and I love your style. I wish I could pull off the innocent, pure look you have. Work it to your favor."

"Thank you so much," Ember replies. "You have the most beautiful clothes in your store, and I can't thank you enough for helping me. I wouldn't have known where to start." She then walks over to where I stand putting my credit card away and wraps her arms around me tightly. "Thank you, Christopher. Thank you for arranging this and for getting me all these clothes and shoes. I needed to get out of the house. I appreciate everything, but—"

"I know," I interrupt. "It's a lot." I kiss her briefly on the lips. "And no need to thank me. We're married now. It's a husband's duty to spoil his wife."

"Oh, it's just the beginning," Christina says. "We're going to enjoy spoiling the hell out of you." She bags up the last of the purchases and looks at her watch. "We finished just in time to head to Luciano's. Michael will be waiting for us with a meal like no other. We need to fatten you both up a little."

I pause and take in the happiness I see on Ember's face. It's a look I've never truly seen before, and a look I plan to make happen every single day.

My captive bride is finally happy. A little taste of freedom is all it takes.

8

EMBER

I'VE NEVER BEEN TO A RESTAURANT BEFORE. LIKE everything with my life, I've read about them, imagined them, but never thought I would actually be inside one, sitting at a table, and about to eat at one.

"Sit, sit, sit," Michael says with more excitement than I've ever seen.

He motions us to a table that has a white tablecloth, candles burning, and place settings waiting for us to eat on. I feel out of place, but his warm smile reminds me of his wife's, and I start to warm up to the situation the minute I realize it's just Christopher, Christina, Michael, and me.

Once we sit down, Michael places his hand on Christopher's shoulder, and his joyous expression morphs to one of seriousness. "It's good to have you back, buddy. It's so fucking good to actually see you here in front of me."

"You aren't going to get all mushy on me now, are ya, Mike?" Christopher teases.

"Asshole," Michael mumbles, but he playfully punches Christopher before announcing, "I have the best pasta dishes made up in the kitchen. I'll be right back."

When he turns to leave, Christina reaches for a bottle of open wine and pours it in all four glasses. Papa Rich didn't believe in drinking—well... he didn't believe in *me* drinking. He would drink hard liquor from time to time, but nothing for me. I'm not about to say anything, however, because I desperately want to fit in. For the first time since we left Hallelujah Junction, I feel somewhat normal in my new clothes and my pair of shoes. I like the way Christopher looks at me.

I like the way I looked at me when I saw my reflection in the mirror.

I no longer look like the ghost of Hallelujah Junction and the daughter of a serial killer.

Michael returns with a large tray full of bowls of different pastas and breads. Unlike how I felt this morning being served by Ms. Evans, this time feels different. This time feels like Michael is getting enjoyment out of cooking and serving the ones he cares about. I like being part of it. I like that I seem to be giving him joy simply by sitting and welcoming his food.

He sits down, picks up his full glass of wine, and raises his glass for a toast. We all lift ours as well, as he says, "To Christopher, for returning to us safe when we had all given up hope. To Ember, for joining our often crazy but very loyal clan of friends. And to friendship. May we never be parted again."

We all tap our glasses, and I sip from the wine as if it isn't the first time for me. I steal a glance at Christopher, who is smiling at me as he drinks. He knows I've never drank wine before, but he seems pleased I'm so willing to try to assimilate to the experience.

"Okay, now that we are seated and eating," Michael begins as we all start digging into the delicious food, "I have *got* to ask some questions. Christina filled me in on everything you told her over the phone, so I understand the back story, but there is so much. It seems so unreal."

Christopher lifts his eyes from his food to me with a look of concern. And though I appreciate it, I'm also comfortable with these people and don't have the feeling of wanting to flee. Even though I just met them, there is something about them that make me feel safe.

"Ask whatever you want," I say, giving a warm smile as reassurance that I mean every word. "I'm sure you are both happy to see your friend return and shocked to see him bring someone back with him."

"What happens now?" Michael asks, and Christina stops chewing to await the answer as well.

"Good question," Christopher says. "Ember and I don't really know. Obviously, I have to start working again, and luckily *Rolling Stone* is interested in having me back. I need to find us a place to live, since my mother sold my apartment, and all of us living under the same roof is something that can only last temporarily. If I don't kill my mother, Ember may," Christopher teases with a wink to me.

"What about you?" Christina asks me. "How is all this for you? It must be a lot to take in, since you've never experienced anything beyond that schoolhouse and town, right?"

"It feels like I'm in a thunderstorm. It's loud. It's windy. It's full of electricity, excitement, but also fear." I lift my wine glass and take another swallow before adding, "I'm happy to have Christopher by my side in all this. I'm also happy to have met the both of you. Your kindness has made a pretty bad day end on a good note."

"So, are you guys really married?" Michael asks.

Christina kicks him under the table not so subtly. "I told you they are."

Christopher nods, reaches over the table, and takes my hand in his. "We are. Far from normal circumstances, but Ember and I have a bond that no one can understand."

Michael chuckles, and he pours himself more wine. "I never thought I'd see you married, bro. Never thought the old ball-and-chain was your style." The minute he said the last sentence, his mouth opened wide, and Christina once again kicks him under the table. "Ah shit, man. Sorry. Poor choice of words."

Christopher laughs... and then continues to laugh so loud and for so long that tears form in the corners of his eyes. "That's fucking funny." He looks at me, and although I didn't catch the joke right at the beginning, I do now. I join in on the laughter until we are all hysterical.

Once the table settles and we're back to eating and drinking, Christina asks, "This might be a sensitive topic, but I'm going to ask anyway. What about Marissa? How is she handling all of it?"

Without even making eye contact with Christopher, I know the question has him tense. I know he's worried how I will respond, so I answer first to try to ease the tension. "She was waiting for us when we arrived yesterday. I know it was really hard for her to see me. To see that Christopher now has a wife. I feel bad for her and wish no one else has to feel pain over actions caused by my father."

"Yeah, it was awkward. Not exactly the homecoming I was expecting," Christopher chimes in. "But a lot has changed since I was last here— one being Marissa. She's a great woman and deserves someone just as great. But... I'm with Ember now. It's not like I planned this or asked for it, but it is the way it is. The past is the past, and we have to move on."

"And your mother?" Michael asks with a smirk. "I'm sure she's loving the attention just as much as she loves having her son back."

Christopher sighs as he takes a large swallow from his drink. "You know my mother well."

Christina pats my hand and says, "You don't let that woman intimidate you. I know she can come across as a cold-hearted bitch, but she's harmless. She can't hurt you."

I feel relief in knowing that others find Louisa Davenport... unlikeable.

"She's trying," Christopher defends. "But she is going insane with the idea of me staying married to Ember."

"What does she want you to do? Throw her out on the street?" Michaels asks, shaking his head. "Wait, don't answer that. I already know the answer."

Christina looks at me and asks, "What about you, Ember? What dreams and hopes do you have? Christopher has his career, but what about you?"

For a minute, I wait for the thunderstorm to return. I wait for the rush of electricity and fear to come, but I'm still at ease and realize Christina isn't judging me or asking out of morbid curiosity. She genuinely seems to care.

I shrug and look around the room as if the answer is waiting for me here within these walls. "I don't know. I never really dreamed of anything before. It wasn't my life. And when Christopher came and we got married, my dream was to be a good wife. It's still my dream. But beyond that, I don't know."

"Do you have any passions? Hobbies?" Michael asks.

"I like to read," I answer. "I also liked to cook, but I could never cook as good as you." I point at the food on my plate. I pause for a moment and add, "But I never dreamed of being anything career wise. I never thought I'd leave Hallelujah Junction. I didn't give myself permission to have hope for anything more than what I already had."

"It's time you start dreaming," Christina says softly as she pats my hand with hers. "The world is yours now. You can have anything you want."

"I think it's going to take Ember awhile to believe that," Christopher says as he leans back in his chair with the wine glass in his hand. He's looking at me with love in his eyes, and heat prickles the back of my neck as his leg brushes mine, and I feel his security and connection flood through me. "Richard messed with her head. He sure as fuck messed with mine. It's going to take us both a bit to get going, but we will."

"Well, if you ever want a job, Ember," Christina chimes in, "the boutique will hire you in a second. I could use the extra help."

"The restaurant too," Michael adds. "If you want to work in the kitchen and around food, I'd love to have you."

"Hey!" Christina teasingly slaps Michael's arms. "Stop trying to steal my employee."

I've never seen this kind of playful banter before, but I like it. I like it a lot.

Friendship.

I know I missed out on a lot of things growing up. I know Papa Rich shielded me from all the world had to offer. I believe that part of him meant well. He was protecting me from all the evil and all the modern society he believed corrupt. But he also kept me from something so very important.

Friendship.

And though I may be wearing shoes for the first time in my life—and yes, I've never drank wine before tonight—the thing that is really standing out to me that I've missed out so much on is that I've never had others care about me simply *because*.

I sit at a table with three people who I don't fear. I don't worry about what they will say or do to me. I don't feel I have to act a certain way or be submissive in every act I do.

For the first time in my life, I feel excited about the future, excited about what's to come.

"I might take you up on the job offer," I say, looking at Christopher to see what he feels about it.

He nods in agreement. "It could be good for you. But first, we need to stop the circus by feeding the animals. We have an interview with *Rolling Stone* tomorrow. My mother's PR person feels it's best to get the story out there in hopes they will grow bored eventually and move on. As long as we keep the mysterious element, they won't go away."

"It's so messed up," Michael grumbles. "You both have enough to deal with right now without all those people hunting you down." He pours us all more wine from the third—maybe fourth—bottle he's opened since the meal began.

Christina lifts her glass to me with a twinkle in her eye. "Wear the blue dress. It will make your eyes pop and your hair shine. I think it will be perfect for the interview, and I know you both will do amazingly."

"Thank you," I say to her. I then look at Michael. "Thank you both. It means a lot to me that you have been so welcoming. I needed this. I didn't know I did, but I feel like I can breathe a little better now."

"We both do," Christopher agrees.

9

CHRISTOPHER

WE TIPTOE INTO THE HOUSE, WHICH I FIND A LITTLE counterproductive, since opening the door allows the noise of the reporters to roar in, but it's late, and I'm hoping my mother is asleep. By the dim lights and the silence inside, it seems that she is.

We make our way to our room and close the door behind us. I don't even have a second once the door clicks before Ember is turning on her heels and wrapping her arms around me.

Pressing her lips to mine, she whispers, "Thank you for tonight. I had the most amazing time."

I kiss her back, dancing my tongue with hers, feeling a little lightheaded from all the wine we drank as my body responds immediately to hers. "I liked seeing you truly smile," I confess. "If I can make that happen every single day, I will."

"My heart feels alive," she says, lowering her hands to my pants, freeing me from my restraints. "I didn't know I could feel this way. My body is buzzing."

She then lifts the dress she'd been wearing over her head, tossing it to the ground. I'm surprised to see her wearing a white lace bra with matching panties. Seeing her in something so normal and everyday fills me with a sense of pride that I can give her such basic things, but they mean the world to her.

"You're beautiful," I say, helping her in our now common goal by lowering my pants as I kick off my shoes and shed my shirt all at the same time.

I like her aggressive act and show of making the first move. Maybe she too is feeling the afterglow of the wine, but it's clear we don't want the night to end quite yet.

"You made me feel special," she says as she runs her finger over my lips, down my neck, over my chest, dipping past my stomach, and then runs a gentle circle over my hard cock. She then removes the last of her clothing.

Pure goddess perfection.

My breath hitches, and my cock aches for more as we're both fully naked and have nothing stopping us from doing more.

I remain standing in place, curious what she has in mind. The girl seems to be on a mission, and I have no intention of stopping her.

Looking up at me through thick lashes, she lowers herself to her knees in front of me. My cock stands at attention before her, and I groan as she takes hold of the base and guides it to her mouth.

"I want to thank you," she purrs as she licks the head of my dick, tasting me, savoring me with her hooded eyes looking up, glazed over in lust.

"I'll take you shopping and to dinner every day if this is the thanks I get," I say as I reach back and find the wall with my palm to help keep my balance.

Her mouth slides down my cock all the way to the base. A tiny gag comes from Ember, which only lights an inferno deeper within my core and with more intensity. I want to tear into the back of her throat with hard pushes but fight the urge and allow her to take control.

Pulling my cock out of her mouth, licking every inch as she does, she whispers, "I want you to do dirty things to me. I don't want to make love. I don't want gentle and loving. I want raw. I want my pussy to feel as alive and buzzing as the rest of my body." She circles her tongue around the tip of my cock again. "Dirty."

"Fuuuck," I barely say on a gasp.

I nearly come at her words. To see my sweet, angelic, naive, innocent Ember nearly growl out these filthy and hot-as-fuck words has me coming undone.

Not thinking, not planning, I take hold of her hair and pull her up to me so I can sink my tongue into her mouth. I want to claim her as mine in all ways. All.

"Get on all fours on the bed," I command.

We have crossed the point of no return. She will do what I say. She will take all the erotic abuse I'm about to give.

With wide eyes, she waits until I release her hair, turns, and obediently does as I ask, sticking her firm ass up on display. She looks over her shoulder at me with vixen blue eyes that make my primal need surge. I crawl up behind her and slap her right ass cheek hard, then the left.

"How dirty?" I hiss.

"Filthy," she answers as she lowers her front half down on her forearms, presenting her ass even more.

My cock twitches in need, but I resist the urge to slam it right inside her with no warning at all.

"Tell me," I order. "Tell me what you want."

"I want you everywhere. I want you to take me where you never have."

I place my finger on her anus and ask, "Where?"

"In my ass," she whispers. "Fuck me in the ass."

I know she's not ready, no matter how much she thinks she is. But that doesn't mean I can't *make* her ready.

"Play with your clit and make yourself nice and wet."

She does exactly as I ask as she balances on one arm and reaches beneath her to stroke her pleasure point with the other. I move my finger from her anus and begin collecting her juices, painting them all over her opening.

"I'm going to stretch you so you can take all of me. It's going to sting. It's going to bite."

"Yes," she moans with a nod, her pussy getting wetter and wetter by the minute. "Yes."

With my finger coated in her arousal, and her asshole nice and slick, I press a finger past the puckered flesh. She whimpers as I do so but doesn't try to wiggle free or break her sexual position even slightly. She simply rubs her clit over and over, her breathing becoming more ragged with each passing second.

In and out, I move my finger, feeling her hole squeeze tightly. It takes everything inside me to not just take her right now.

"Wetter," I say as I dip a second finger in her pussy, soaking the skin.

Not waiting, I push the second finger into her ass, joining the other.

She cries out but pushes back toward my hand. I can see she doesn't want me to stop even though I'm spreading her wider than she can handle and still remain quiet. I don't mind her cries; in fact, they make my dick harder with each mewl that passes her lips.

"Does it hurt?" I ask as I lean forward and kiss the taut skin of her ass.

"Yes," she cries. "But I like it. I want more. I want you."

Unable to control myself any longer, I quickly get off the bed and pull some lubrication out of the bedside table. This isn't going to be easy.

Slicking my dick, I retake my position behind her and position myself at her back entrance. "I'll try to take this as slowly as I can." Though I don't know if this is a promise I can keep.

The minute I breech the entrance, Ember squeals, tenses, but doesn't tell me to stop.

I push a little farther, pausing so she can adjust to the size of me and the stretch. The tightness around me nearly makes me come, but I'm determined to be buried balls-deep before I do.

"Keep playing with that clit," I coach. "Relax and take deep breaths."

Like a good student, she does exactly that, moaning and eventually pressing her ass against me, driving me even deeper inside.

"Fuck me," she coos. "Fuck my ass, Christopher. I don't want you to hold back."

Grasping her hips, I begin pushing and pulling her forward and back. I inch my way deeper each time, claiming her ass as she had so animalistically begged me to do.

Sweat glistens on her lower back, and her moans grow in intensity until a shudder works over every inch and every muscle of her body. The tightness in her ass convulses around my cock, and no matter how hard I try to fight it back, I explode in her ass with a roar of passion.

She collapses onto her stomach with me falling on top of her, my cock still firmly planted inside her ass. I give her tiny kisses on her neck, on her shoulder, on her upper back.

"You've got a hidden vixen inside this innocent body of yours," I pant as I regain composure.

"You bring it out in me." She giggles as goose bumps cover her skin caused by my kisses. "I liked the wine. It made me... hungry."

I chuckle as I finally pull out of her and roll onto my back, staring at the ceiling. "Clearly." I turn my head to look at her wild hair and satiated eyes. "I'm going to make sure the wine cellar stays fully stocked."

10

WE SIT ACROSS FROM A REPORTER WITH *ROLLING Stone.* Christopher tried to prep me the best he could before today, but I know he doesn't think I'm ready. He never thinks I'm ready, and maybe he's right. But I can only speak my truth. He told me that the reporter will see right through me if I lie. He told me the reporter will eat me up and spit me out if he even for a second feels I'm not being genuine. He also told me that if I'm uncomfortable with a question, then to simply say I'm not comfortable answering, but if that were the case, I wouldn't answer a thing. I can't see how I'll be comfortable speaking about my father who everyone thinks is a villain, and who I think is either haunting or stalking me now.

"Hello, Ember, Christopher. Thank you for joining me today."

Rolling Stone doesn't usually do television interviews, but they decided to shoot the interview as well in case they want to sell the story to a network to air. They're covering all their bases. From what Jason told us, there's going to be a bidding war from the networks.

We're surrounded by large lights, big reflectors, and three different cameras placed in strategic areas to get all three of us as we speak. I'm happy Jason took hours prepping Christopher on what exactly to say and what not to say. I could tell it frustrated Christopher, but I know I needed it. This entire process scares me. I don't want to mess it up for us. I want to be able to move on, and Christopher believes this is the only way to do that.

"Do either of you have any questions before we start?" he asks.

"Let's just get this over with," Christopher says as a woman runs a makeup brush over my cheeks and the tip of my nose again.

When another man by the camera signals it's time to start, the reporter begins by introducing us and giving a brief description of our story. I try to tune out all the words he's saying the best that I can. I hate hearing how Papa Rich hit Christopher from behind with a mallet, kidnapped, and chained him up in the cellar. I also hate that they refer to him as a serial killer who murdered dozens by pushing them to their deaths in the acid pits of the mill. It sounds so awful and makes him worse than the devil. And though I know deep down he's all they say and did everything mentioned... I still hate hearing him spoken of in this way.

He tells the story of how we burned down Hallelujah Junction, and I'm ashamed we destroyed something so beautiful and so rich and full of history. That town was there long before us, and yet we ruined it all. I can't help but feel that it was the most selfish act we could have done. I know we were escaping, but I hate the fact that those ashes left behind are because of me.

"So, Ember. Let's start with you. Is it true you lived with Richard since you were five years old?"

"Yes," I say softly but then remember Christopher coaching me only minutes ago to speak loud and clear. To show confidence, even if I'm not feeling it. "I went to live with him when I was five. My memory is fuzzy around that time."

"Did he kidnap you?"

"I don't think so. I don't remember being afraid or feeling like I was kept against my will. But like I said, it's all a bit fuzzy around that time. It's like another lifetime ago."

"Did he change your name from Amber to Ember? Isn't your real name Amber Jennings?"

"I guess so, maybe?" I say with a shrug. "Or maybe I told him Ember. I don't really remember, to be honest. I've always known my name to be Ember, and I never knew what my last name was."

The reporter pauses as if he's carefully watching my every move and analyzing my every word. I feel like he's waiting for me to mess up somehow so he can pounce and not have to be so polite with me. He finally continues with "When he kidnapped you, did he keep you chained in the basement like he did Christopher?"

Memories of the times he did lock me in the cellar —for my own sake—come flooding in. "Yes, sometimes. But mostly, I stayed in the schoolhouse during the days and walked underground in the tunnels to the main house. He wanted me to stay out of sight from everyone. He told me that my life was in danger, and he was keeping me safe from those who wanted to do me harm."

"Who wanted to do you harm?"

"He told me that my mother did. I believed him."
The look the reporter gives me makes me uneasy. I
can't tell if he thinks I'm stupid or is showing a look
of pity.

"Did you ever think of escaping?"

I look at Christopher briefly, and he simply nods
his encouragement for me to answer and keep the
interview moving along. "No."

"Was it because you were afraid of him?" the
reporter asks.

Honest.

Be honest.

But what if Papa Rich will read the interview or see
me on television? What will he say? How will he
react if I tell the reporter my truth?

Be honest.

"Yes, I guess I was. I was afraid of what he would
do. I witnessed what happened when people broke
his rules. I didn't want it to happen to me, so I
followed his rules no matter what they were."

"Are you talking about the acid pits? How he brought innocent people to the mill and pushed them to their deaths while you watched?"

"She was a child," Christopher defends. "She was brainwashed to believe that Papa Rich knew best. And there was nothing she could do to stop it. I saw it in full action. The man was demented and frankly not someone you wanted to cross."

The reporter turns his attention to Christopher, which allows me to breathe out a sigh of relief. "And did you witness him killing people in the same way?"

"Sadly, yes," Christopher says. "Ember and I came close to escaping one other time, and a young man and woman were trying to help us. We came close but failed. Richard took the couple to the pits and made us watch as he pushed them to their deaths. He then threw Ember's cat into the pit to punish her even more."

I snapped my eyes toward Christopher, angry he's bringing up my dead cat, Pine Cone. There's no need to discuss my cat. It's a detail that doesn't need to be said, and it stabs my heart and rips out my soul, having to relive that awful memory.

"There are reports that you and Ember are married. That Richard had a pastor come to the property and marry you. Is that true?" the reporter continues. I wonder where he's getting all his information and am angry our personal business is so easy to come by.

"Yes, Ember and I are married. The entire reason I wasn't killed in the pit like the other victims was that Richard wanted me to marry Ember—who he considered his daughter. He treated it like an old-fashioned arranged marriage."

"So let me get this straight," the reporter says, shaking his head as if it will help him make sense of our twisted tale. "You were kidnapped, chained in a cellar, and then forced to marry the woman who this man kidnapped as a child. A woman who had been hidden away in a ghost town?"

Christopher reaches out and pats my knee as he nods in agreement. "I know it's hard to believe. I think one of the most difficult things about being held captive was trying to come to terms that the nightmare was real. That the man was truly serious and believed he was acting under God in his decisions. There was no reasoning with him. There was no way I could threaten, bribe, or even plead my way out of it."

"Why would Richard want you to marry his daughter? Why?"

"He loved me," I say flatly. "He wanted the best for me. Family, old-fashioned values, God, and... regardless of what he did, he did have a strong belief in those. And he loved me."

"Love?" The reporter raises an eyebrow and smirks. "You call locking you away from civilization for your entire life love?"

I nod, confident in my statement. "Yes, because in his mind, modern civilization is dangerous, corrupt, and sinful. He saw it as protecting me. When he killed all those people... he justified it as a show of love. Protection."

"I saw it with my own eyes," Christopher adds. "The man truly saw Ember as his daughter. But he was so sick and twisted. His level of control via fear is what made it so hard to escape."

"Ember," the reporter redirects his attention to me, "did you help him kill those people?"

I don't even have a chance to open my mouth before Christopher snaps, "She was as much a victim as them. She was a child who had to grow up as a prisoner for her entire life. She was forced to witness awful acts that will stay with her forever. Of course she didn't help kill those people. Richard was a madman. He was a killer, and Ember is lucky to finally be free of him. She is finally free."

The reporter seems satisfied with the answer, because he changes topic slightly. "Yes, let's talk about free," he says. "Ember, if you have been locked away for most of your life, what's it like to be *free*? How are you adjusting?"

"It's scary," I say softly but then clear my throat before speaking loudly again. "I've read about a lot of this stuff—life—but to actually see it, hear it... it's scary."

"Ember is adjusting well. It's going to be a slow process, and we're trying to introduce her to modern society in baby steps," Christopher adds. "My family, friends, and I plan to be with her every step of the way."

"And what about you?" the reporter asks. "You've been gone for months. I'm sure there were points in captivity that you feared you may never be free again. How are you adjusting to being back?"

"It's a process too," Christopher admits. "I'm starting to get back to work, trying to get my normal routine back. But that man, Richard, really messed with me." He looks at me and takes my hand in his. "My focus is primarily on Ember right now, however. I feel this need to protect her, even though mentally she's by far the strongest person I've ever met."

My heart feels as if it erupts in happiness. Strong? Christopher considers me strong?

He's complimented me many times, but nothing is so rewarding as hearing the word *strong*. I've never been one to think that is a word to describe me, and yet Christopher believes it does.

The reporter nods as if he too agrees I'm strong and then asks, "Is it true Richard could still be alive and on the run? Do you believe he's still out there?"

I think the reporter is asking me, but Christopher answers. "When Ember and I were leaving the burning town, we saw Richard run into the main house, which was engulfed in flames. We assumed he died but were later told they never found his body. So yes. He could still be alive, and he could still be out there."

"Are you afraid of your 'Papa Rich'?" the reporter asks me. "Are you afraid he may find you again and take you back? He's a serial killer. Do you fear he may come to you and Christopher and finish the job?"

I notice that the reporter used the name Papa Rich rather than Richard, and I don't know why. But regardless, I answer, "He can be a very dangerous man."

Even admitting the words has me trembling. This is the most I've had to think of Richard and my past since arriving in New York, and I'm reaching my max. I hate hearing him be referred to as a serial killer, even though I suppose in definition he is.

He killed a lot of people.

Not once. Not twice. A lot.

So many screams and people begging for their lives. So many innocent lives gone forever.

I need air. I need a break. I need to stop being looked at like I'm a zoo animal.

"Ember, did Papa Rich ever abuse you?

"He was a very strict man."

"Did he ever sexually abuse you?"

My face heats at the thought. How could someone think such a thing, and yet... Papa Rich did bad, bad things. "No."

He looks at Christopher. "Richard forced you to marry Ember. Did he also force you to consummate the marriage?"

"I'm not comfortable answering this question," Christopher says calmly. "Intimate details about Ember and me are private."

The reporter is clearly not happy with the answer. "Were you expected to be married as a true husband and wife would be? Did Richard want children to come from the marriage?"

This isn't right. We shouldn't be talking about... sex. It's sinful. It's wrong.

"Can we take a moment?" Christopher asks, clearly picking up on my emotions and the tension in my body.

The reporter looks at the camera and says, "Cut." He then looks at me. "We'll take a little break. Let you get up and stretch your legs for a sec. You're both doing great. Only a few more questions."

The reporter is the first to stand, and I watch him take out a package of cigarettes and walk to a door with an exit sign shining in green light above it.

"You are doing great," Christopher praises as he kisses me softly on the cheek. "I'm proud of you."

"Do you really think the media will leave us alone after we do this interview?" I hate every part of this day, but if it means the people out front of the house will go away, I'll do anything.

"Maybe not at first, but the big scoop will be covered. Eventually, a new story will hit that will pull them away from us. Jason's right in pushing for us to do this. I hate having my business out on full display too, but if it means we can eventually get back to normal, then so be it."

Normal.

Will I ever know what *normal* is supposed to be?

It's not long before the reporter is back and ready to go. Christopher and I had a chance to use the restroom and get a drink of water, but nothing more. I'm happy that not a lot of time passed, because I want this over with as fast as possible.

Not wasting any time, the reporter dives back in the minute we are all sitting and the camera's red light is on. "There are a lot of families looking for answers right now about their loved ones who died in Hallelujah Junction. Have the authorities used you in identifying the victims, Ember?"

I nod. "I tried to help them the best that I could. But when it all happened—the acid pits—I tried not to look. I tried to close my eyes and block it all out. I don't remember the faces as much as the authorities hoped I would. It's awful what happened. I just hope the families can finally find some peace. Closure maybe?"

"Richard deserves to pay for what he did," Christopher says. "Ember and I will both cooperate with the FBI in any way we can. If he didn't die in that fire, then we hope he's caught, and justice can be served."

The reporter points to the camera. "Ember, if Richard is watching right now, what would you say to him?"

I look at the camera, at the reporter, and then back at the camera. I don't know what to say. Maybe I have nothing to say. Maybe words can't express my thoughts. But I know the reporter is waiting. The men behind and next to the camera are waiting. I have to say something. Swallowing hard, I say in the loudest and most confident voice I can somehow muster, "You were wrong. What you did, what you said, and what you believed... wrong. You were wrong."

The reporter then asks Christopher the exact same question. Christopher, however, doesn't take as long to answer as I did. "Richard... if you're out there and you're watching, just know one thing. I'll find you. You'll pay for what you did to me, to all the innocent people who died, and to Ember. I'm coming for you."

11

EMBER

I LOOK DOWN BELOW AND NOTICE THE CROWDS OF reporters are getting smaller and smaller each day that passes. Jason was right when he said they would grow bored and we would be old news after the *Rolling Stone* interview. I know Christopher is happy about it; he seems more relaxed and able to go to work without having to fight through a wave of madness.

A knock on the door has broken my thoughts, and I turn as Ms. Evans pops her head in. "Ember? I'm sorry for just opening the door—I've been knocking."

"Oh sorry. I must have been lost in thought," I say, not sure how long I've been staring out the window.

"I've come to tell you that Christopher called and said he won't be home for dinner. But Mrs. Davenport is joining you tonight. It will be done soon, so you should come downstairs. Mrs. Davenport likes the meal and her guests prompt."

I'm surprised to hear I'll be having dinner with Louisa... alone. I haven't seen much of her since arriving. Christopher told me she's extremely busy with all her social engagements, but I also get the feeling she avoids me. Looking down at my bare feet, dreading putting shoes on, I wish she'd still avoid me—especially with Christopher not being here. I'm used to him working late, and have gotten accustomed to eating alone, but now... I'm not ready for dinner with Louisa.

Taking Ms. Evans's advice, I freshen up, put on the awful shoes that make my feet feel like they are being strangled, and make my way to the dining room. Louisa is already sitting at the head of the table, her palms resting on the polished wood. Candles are lit, fine china and silverware adorn the place settings, and crystal glasses are already poured with wine. It's been like this every night, as it's the rule of the Davenport household to have formal dinners, but for some reason, having Louisa present makes it even fancier.

"Glad you could make it on time," she says, but based on her glare at me, I feel like I'm tardy even though I came straight down.

"I didn't know I'd be having dinner with you," I say as I quickly sit down, grateful to have her not examining my outfit any longer, since I can hide beneath the expansive table. "But I'm happy that I am. I've been eating alone all week with Christopher being back at work now."

"Yes," she says as she sips her wine, her eyes focusing in on me over the glass. "At least he was able to get his job back. With all the negative attention he's getting, I'm so happy the magazine is willing to look past it. Of course, as you know, he doesn't *have* to work. Being a Davenport allows him comforts in life if he chose to take them. But he's a proud man."

We sit in awkward silence until Ms. Evans serves us roasted chicken and vegetables. I wish she'd sit down and join us, but I already learned it isn't the role she plays, and there are no exceptions.

"How are you adjusting?" She finally cuts the silence. "I'm sure living in such a large house compared to where you came from has to be... foreign."

"You have a lovely house. I've walked around and really love all the artwork you have."

"Yes, Christopher's father, my late husband, was a collector."

"Christopher told me that once I get a passport, we can travel to places with museums and galleries. I want to actually see all the art I've read about."

Louisa places her glass on the table and finally takes her first—very dainty—bite of chicken. "Do you really see that happening?"

Confused by the question, I ask, "What do you mean?"

"Travel. With Christopher. Do you really think you will ever be ready to do such a... normal task?"

I don't know if her question is meant to be an insult, but it certainly feels as if it's one.

"I hope so," I say, deciding to not make an issue of the question. "I know Christopher is busy with work right now, so I know it's still a ways out. Plus, we need to start looking for a place to live. He told me last night that he'd arrange for us to meet with a real estate agent soon."

"Do you think that's a good idea? Who will take care of you when he's at work? Ms. Evans and I won't be present."

"I don't feel I need to be taken care of." I look to the door leading to the kitchen. "The only reason I don't cook for myself, and even for the entire household, is because Christopher told me it's Ms. Evans's domain, and I could upset her if I do." Lowering my eyes to the dinner presentation, guilt attacks. Had I made a mistake in listening to Christopher? "I'd be more than happy to do more around the house if you'd like."

"That won't be necessary. It's not about the housework. I'm referring to your mental state."

"Excuse me?" I'm fighting back the urge to stand up and storm out of the room. Not only is the conversation attacking in nature, but it's awkward and uncomfortable. I don't know how to respond properly, nor am I sure if I'm just being overly sensitive and reading her questions the wrong way.

"Come now, Amber," she says as she dabs the corner of her mouth with a linen napkin. "You are essentially a caged animal that has been released. It's not natural or even expected for you to behave in normal society after the upbringing you've had."

"Ember," I correct, trying to ignore her calling me a caged animal.

"In my house, we go by our proper birth-given names." Her face is emotionless, cold, and full of disgust. This woman doesn't like me, and even a *caged animal* can see that.

I poke my fork into a carrot and try not to respond while anger bubbles from my stomach to the back of my throat.

"Let me ask you something," she says after a few moments of silence.

"Yes?" I look at her, readying myself for a bullet to the heart. I can feel she's going in for the kill.

"How was your wedding? I ask because it's a mother's dream to be part of her son's wedding. To dance with him on his special night. To be part of the planning. To witness the vows to the new woman in his life. I had none of that. You stole that from me. So, tell me... how was your wedding?"

"I... I'm sorry."

"Tell me. I'd like to know."

"It was just Christopher, Papa Rich, me, and Scarecrow. It wasn't really a wedding. No cake or anything."

She gives a sickly smile. "No cake? Oh, what a shame."

"Louisa—"

"Mrs. Davenport," she snaps. "You have not earned the position to call me by my first name."

Again, I'm only doing what Christopher said, but I decide it best to not argue or point out that her son disagrees.

"Mrs. Davenport," I say evenly. "I'm sorry that my marriage to your son is upsetting. I completely understand why it would be. I wish things were different and that it didn't happen the way it did."

"Then end it," she blurts. "It's quite simple. It's not legal, and my attorney doesn't even have to draw up any papers to divorce. You simply have to walk away." She raises her hand when I open my mouth to object. "I'm not expecting you to just walk out of my house with nothing. In fact, I can be very generous and will be if you choose to go. I can set you up in an apartment and give you a nice little bank account that allows you to live comfortably. All I will ask in return is that you stay away from Christopher. You don't have any contact with him from this point on. I can have assistants here within the hour to take you away. I can make it very easy for you and have them handle it all."

"He's my husband."

"No, Amber, he isn't."

"I'm not going to leave Christopher. I'm sorry. I'm not."

"Then you're just as bad as Richard. He may have forced you both to get married, but *you* are forcing it to continue. My son was a victim of your father. But you, Amber, are torturing him more than Richard ever did."

I shake my head, tears escaping my eyes no matter how hard I try to fight them off. "That's not true. I live every single day to make Christopher happy. I love him. He loves me."

She laughs. A laugh so evil it sends a shiver down my spine. "He doesn't love you. He feels obligated. You are his responsibility. He brought home a stray and now has to feed and house it. It's not love. Understand that. It's far from love. You can't force love, and that is exactly what you and Richard did to him."

I push away from the table and drop my napkin on the plate. "I'm sorry. I've lost my appetite."

Without waiting to be excused or allowing the conversation to continue, I spin on my heels and march up the stairs. I'm careful not to run. I take each step evenly and slowly. I don't want to seem hysterical and out of control. I want to scream and yell. Actually, I really wanted to throw my wine glass at the woman's head but restrained myself.

Her words sting so badly it feels like a nest full of hornets is attacking my heart, shredding my soul.

Is she right?

Does Christopher not really love me?

Am I nothing but a stray dog that has just been let out of her cage?

12

CHRISTOPHER

"You missed dinner," I hear to my left when I walk into the house.

I enter the dining room and see my mother sitting at the head of the table, sipping her wine. Her half-eaten plate still sits in front of her as well as another barely touched plate, which I assume was Ember's. She hadn't had much of an appetite since arriving, and I make a mental note to keep an eye on how little she is eating. She's tiny enough to begin with, and I need to make sure she keeps up her strength.

I pick up a potato and pop it into my mouth as I lean against the back of Ember's chair. "Shoot ran long," I say. "Sorry."

"Sit," she says as she motions for me to sit. "I'll have Ms. Evans bring you out your dinner."

"I'm fine," I say. "I ate at the shoot."

"Still... sit."

I can see she's serious, and I decide to humor and give her some time. I hadn't had any real alone time with her since arriving and figured she'd like some with me without all the crazy media, and even without Ember.

As soon as I sit, she begins. "I'd like to talk about your future."

I nod. "I know. I'm working on it. Ember and I will be out of your hair as soon as we find a place. I've been so busy, and with everything going on, I didn't feel it was right to just dive right in. I don't want to move Ember from one rental to another, so I'm looking at buying a place. I want it to be just right and not settle."

"When will you stop with the dutiful husband act?" Her words come out like sharp glass, slicing at my calm and relaxed mood I had been in when entering the house.

I sigh loudly and reach for the bottle of wine, pouring Ember's glass full so I can have a little liquid courage for what I know will be a conversation that won't end well.

"Go ahead," I say. "Tell me how I'm making a mistake. How I'm ruining my life. How I need to kick Ember out on her ass. Get it out of your system so I don't ever have to hear you say this shit again."

"It's all true. You just said it, because you know deep down it's true."

"Wonderful. Are we done?" My jaw locks as I take deep breaths to try to keep my cool.

"No, far from it. Have you even tried calling Marissa? That poor girl deserves a phone call. I know she's trying to be understating and give you space, but you should be putting her feelings into consideration. Have you even tried reaching out?"

Clearly, my mother already knows the answer to that question, or she wouldn't be asking. "No. I need time. I will when I'm ready."

"She was your girlfriend. You loved her. Is this how she deserves to be treated?"

"Of course not," I snap. "I know I need to face her and deal with this, but it's not exactly easy. And it's not as if I haven't had my hands full. Call it selfish, but my bandwidth can only handle so much right now. But yes, I plan on talking to Marissa. She deserves closure."

"Why closure? Why can't you be with her? Just because you went through an ordeal doesn't mean you have to stop loving her. She was marriage material. You and she both had something great, and I knew she'd be the perfect wife. Her social standing matches yours, and together, you can really be a power couple. She'd be good for your reputation and career. She's worthy of the Davenport name."

"We were not going to get married, Mother. Not even close. I was so far from thinking about marriage—"

"And yet you marry *her*!" my mother cuts in.

"I told you. I didn't have a choice. I had to do what I had to do and say what I had to say to survive. I had to plan my escape and outsmart Richard. I told you all this."

"And yet, you are still with her. You don't have to be."

I pinch the bridge of my nose and close my eyes. "She's my wife. I've chosen to stay with her. I want this. I want to be married to her. I know it's hard for you to understand—"

"It's insanity! I don't think you're thinking clearly."

I put down the glass of wine I consider downing in one gulp before I reach for the bottle and finish it off in seconds, but I don't. "That's just it. I'm finally thinking clearly for the first time in a very, very long time. Before I was kidnapped, a single day didn't go by that I didn't drink or pop pills. My camera bag was a traveling pharmacy. I was under one form of influence or another since I can remember."

Her lips twitch, but her eyes remain steadfast on me. She's prepared for battle, and nothing I say is going to rattle her, but I'm going to be brutally honest.

"I know you think that me being chained in a cellar was my darkest moment in life. In all actuality, the life I was living before it was far darker. In many ways, Ember saved me. She didn't just help me escape Richard, but she helped me escape the spiral of booze and pills I was in."

"You weren't that bad," she counters.

"You saw what you wanted to see." I push the wine away just to prove to myself that I can. "I'm a different man now. And yes, I know I'm fucked up from everything that happened and have a lot to deal with in regards to that. But there is a bright light that came from it all, and it's Ember. It's also that I walked away with a new outlook on life. I want to be a better man. I want to provide and protect that woman upstairs. I want to take care of her and put her needs before my own. Which frankly, Mother, makes me a new man. The old Christopher only thought of himself and no one else. I came first. Me and only me."

"She's trapped you," my mother says simply as she takes a sip of her wine, leans back in her chair, and crosses her legs. She is still poised for the battle to continue. "Richard did it first, and she followed. She's no better than him."

"No," I say softly as I shake my head. "She's given me hope. I'm looking forward to our future. And if you want to know the painful truth, it's that I'm finally happy. I don't know how long it's been since I've felt that. Yes, my life is in chaos, but she's my lifeboat. I need you to try to understand that. I need you to give that woman upstairs some understanding. I get it. I know she doesn't have the social graces and status you're used to me bringing home—"

"You've brought home a mangey mutt!"

I scoot my chair back and glare at her as I do. "I'm not going to sit here any longer and allow you to attack my *wife*. My wife!"

She swallows hard to simmer the rage she just released. "I'm trying to make you see reason, Christopher. You have a woman who, though is very sweet and innocent, is also sick. She needs mental help that we are unable to give. I have a list of some very well-respected hospitals that are willing to accept her. Of course they will give her her own room, and I'll make all the arrangements. We can keep this extremely discreet."

"Are you kidding me?" I hiss. "Are you suggesting we commit Ember to a mental institute? Please tell me you aren't saying this."

"I've heard her crying out at night with the bad dreams. I see the way she stares off and is lost in thought. With what she's been through, this could be very good for her. She needs to be in a safe environment where she can learn how to survive in the real world. She has demons and ghosts haunting her, and she always will. You're strong, Christopher, but not strong enough to handle this. To handle her. You would be doing her a favor."

"Do you hear yourself? How is committing my wife to a loony bin doing her a favor?"

"Because she needs the help. She may never be able to heal unless we give her the assistance to do so. She needs someone who specializes in abductions like this. I've been doing some research. We can have them come to her here to take her away. They can do it all without hysterics and drama. They can convince her it's for her own good, because it is! It's for her own good!"

"This conversation is over." I turn to leave before I say something I'll regret.

"Christopher," she calls before I can get away. "I'm asking you to consider this. Think on it. If she goes away to get some help, and you both have some time apart... well... if you still think being with her afterward is a good idea, then I will give my full blessing in the union."

"Good thing I'm not asking for your blessing. Now, if you'll excuse me, I'm going to see my wife."

13

"Ms. Evans?" I call out as I peek my head into the kitchen. "Are you in here?" I'm afraid to fully enter her domain without asking permission.

"Ember?" She walks into my view with a look of confusion on her face. She's wiping her hands with a dishtowel as she approaches. "Is everything all right? Are you hungry? I noticed you didn't eat much for lunch. Would you like me to fix you a snack?"

I push the door open wider and enter. "Is it okay if I come in?"

Ms. Evans seems surprised by my question. "Of course." She takes a few steps backward to the massive kitchen island.

I see a large pot on the stove, which is at least three times the size of the stove I had in my kitchen, and I wonder what wonderful meal she's preparing.

"I was wondering if I could help you with dinner," I say, nervous to do something that could upset the woman if what Christopher said was true. "It's just that... I'm used to cooking."

Ms. Evans smiles and points to the carrots lying on the chopping block. "I don't have much left, but you can help me by chopping the carrots."

Relief washes over me. I quickly pick up the knife and begin before the woman can change her mind.

She returns her attention to the pot on the stove and begins adding different seasonings in the bubbling liquid.

"Thank you," I say, focusing on my task. "With Christopher at work all the time now, I'm starting to get a little stir crazy. The walls are closing in on me."

"You should get out and go for a walk. Take in the sights," she suggests.

"I've thought of doing that. Especially since the media outside doesn't seem as crazy anymore. But all I see is concrete. Buildings. People. It makes me miss Hallelujah Junction. Which I know must sound crazy. But I miss the sounds of nature." I'm not sure why I'm confessing all my feelings. Maybe it's being in a kitchen doing familiar tasks, but the honesty floods out of me. "I wouldn't know where to go."

"Hmm," Ms. Evans says as she walks over to where I stand and leans against the island. "You should go to Central Park. I think you'd love it there. It's a little piece of nature in all this city. It's beautiful and could be just the fresh setting you need right now."

"Sounds lovely, but Christopher wants me to stay close to home, and we have supper to cook, and—"

"Forget about dinner. It's on autopilot now, and besides, I get paid to worry about it. Not you. And don't you dare tell Christopher this, but I think he's hovering over you a little. I think you can handle yourself just fine to go for a little walk. An adventure will do you good." She taps her finger on her chin. "You like books, right?"

I nod, unsure why I'm getting excited at the idea of leaving when I know Christopher wouldn't like it one bit.

"There's an *Alice in Wonderland* statue at the park. Just like the book. I think you'll love it. I always do. And if I weren't on shift right now, I'd take you." She pauses and studies me. "But I also think this little bit of independence can do you good. Because you're right. You've been holed up in this house for days. It's not healthy. You need to stretch your legs and soul a bit."

She's right. I have been locked away. Just like I was locked away in the schoolhouse.

No.

Things will be different this time.

I won't be locked away.

And I want desperately to prove to Christopher that he doesn't have to watch over me every second. That I'm capable of doing things on my own and becoming a functioning adult in this new world.

"I love *Alice in Wonderland*. It's one of my favorites."

"Then it's decided," Ms. Evans says as she walks over to a counter that is holding a phone. "You go get ready, and I'll call a car for you."

Before I change my mind, I do exactly that and rush out of the kitchen, prepared to show everyone who worries if I can ever be

independent that they are wrong. I can do this.
I can.

The eyes of Alice stare back at me. The statue is bigger and more magnificent than I could have imagined. The Mad Hatter and the hare... I want to touch it, but I'm not sure if I should. A bronze Alice perched high on a giant mushroom, surrounded by the Mad Hatter and the White Rabbit as he checks his pocket watch. Engraved around the base of the statue, there are parts of a poem that stand out to me most:

He took his vorpal sword in hand;

Long time the manxome foe he sought—

So rested he by the Tumtum tree

And stood awhile in thought.

And, as in uffish thought he stood,

The Jabberwock, with eyes of flame,

Came whiffling through the tulgey wood,

And burbled as it came!

.   .   .

One, two! One, two! And through and through

The vorpal blade went snicker-snack!

He left it dead, and with its head

He went galumphing back.

"And hast thou slain the Jabberwock?

Come to my arms, my beamish boy!

O frabjous day! Callooh! Callay!"

He chortled in his joy.

Ms. Evans was right about the park giving me a piece of nature I so desperately missed. I needed fresh air. I needed to see and hear birds. I needed to see trees and grass and not just buildings and roads. But my heart also beats so fast and furious that I struggle to breathe normally. The driver of the car promised to wait for me, so at least I know there is a way to return home, but being so far away nearly makes my knees buckle. What if something happens? What if I can't reach Christopher?

I clutch my cell phone in my pocket as a reminder that I'm only a phone call away.

There are people here. Lots of people, but they aren't looking at me. They're busy. They are preoccupied with themselves. So in many ways, I'm alone, even though I'm within arm's reach of strangers.

I take a few steps to the right of the statue so I can see it from another angle. I relate to Alice. I too have gone down my own rabbit hole. I'm in a Wonderland of my own. A mad, mad world where everything is foreign and different. But I'm coming out of it stronger. I have to believe that.

Each day that passes feels better. I'm starting to feel as if I'm no longer the scared little girl in the schoolhouse. I know I have a long ways to go, but coming here by myself, in an expansive park I've never been in, I'm proving this to myself.

I love Christopher, but I don't want to need him.

I want him to love me but not feel he has to shield me from everything.

Alice found her own way in Wonderland by herself. She was strong... and so am I. I can do this. I can find my own way. I have to. I want to.

"One of my favorite parts of Central Park," a man's voice says beside me. "It's nice to see someone else take the time to appreciate it like I do."

I turn to find an elderly man standing next to me, staring at the statue like I was.

"I didn't expect it to be so big," I say.

"First time?" he asks. "Where are you traveling from?"

"I live here now. I'm trying to learn the city and was told to start here."

"Wise choice, and welcome. I've lived here most of my life. New York is the best place to live in the world, but I'm biased." He chuckles. "Where are you from?"

I don't know what to say. I don't want to lie, but I can't exactly be honest either. Then it dawns on me. I'll never be able to truly talk about my past with anyone. That part of my life died, and I have no choice but to try to push it out of my mind. I can't talk about my childhood. I can't share memories neither good nor bad. I have to start over.

Unlike Alice, I have no home to return to. I can't leave the rabbit hole. I'm in it now. I'm always in it. This isn't a dream I can wake up from.

"You know," the man continues when I never answer his question, "Alice is considered to have paranoid schizophrenia, and the Mad Hatter being bipolar. There are even mental illness syndromes named after them. I don't know if everyone knows that, but it's true."

I tilt my head and look at the statue through different eyes with the little-known fact. "I can relate with Alice. Everything in her life was so... big. Or small. I feel that way sometimes. Nothing is the right size around me."

"I know who you are," the man says. "I feel I should be forthcoming and tell you that. I don't know why I acted like I didn't."

"I'm sure I stand out," I say, not feeling uncomfortable by his confession. Maybe I should, but I don't. "And I understand why you wouldn't want to act like you know who I am. I get it."

"You know, I can relate with you in some ways," he replies.

I turn my head and look at him. "How?"

"I was a prisoner of war for years. I served in the Korean War. Held captive for so long that I lost time. And when I was eventually rescued and returned to the land of the living... well, I felt like everything was either too big or too small as well. I felt more captive than I ever did before. Sometimes I missed my prison. At least in my prison, I knew what to expect. I had learned my prison. It was part of me. Being free didn't always feel free."

I don't say anything but stare at the statue again, examining the parts of the artwork that have been polished to a smoothness that nearly erases the texture of the surface. The man seems to say exactly what I'm feeling. I don't think anyone would understand me if I told them I miss not being able to leave the schoolhouse.

I miss my cat.

I miss what I considered my home.

I miss Papa Rich and knowing his schedule.

I miss watching the tourists from afar.

I liked knowing I was safe behind the **No Trespassing** signs. Now, there are no signs to keep me safe.

"How did you deal with it?" I ask. "How did you find your place again?"

"I didn't for a really long time. And if I'm being honest, I'm always a little off the normal path others walk. I tried to fit in the perfect bubble, but it suffocated me. Therapy helped, and I sometimes still go. I think it will always be there to haunt me. But I can tell you it does get easier with time. It's also okay to accept yourself for the way you are. You're different. You experienced a different life. There's no way anyone can truly understand you except you. So, love yourself. Be patient with yourself. Give yourself the grace you need to heal. Now that you are away from the enemy, you're going to realize the real enemy is you."

"I want to be normal. I don't want to be different," I confess. "And it's hard to love myself. I wish I could just be like everyone else. I wish the nightmares would disappear. But they don't. No matter what I do, they are here. And not just when I'm asleep. I have waking nightmares."

"That's okay. I had them too. I sometimes still do, but they ease too."

"I hope so. I really do."

"Embrace who you are. It's taken me a long time to be able to do that myself. You're young and will eventually find your way."

We stand in silence for several minutes, both staring at the bronze sculpture.

"I really should be going," I say, feeling as if others are starting to recognize who I am, and it's just a matter of time until pictures are taken and the media arrives.

The elderly man nods. "Thank you for taking the time to listen to the ramblings of an old man. You have a nice evening. And enjoy New York. I think you'll like it here."

"Thank you for your kind words and advice," I say as I scurry away and head back to the car.

Christopher

"What do you mean she's gone?" I demand when Ms. Evans tells me Ember isn't home.

"She was getting a little cabin fever," the woman explains calmly, when I'm feeling anything but. "She went to Central Park."

"Central Park? Alone? Are you fucking kidding me? How did she get there? Whose idea was this? Ms. Evans! You were supposed to keep an eye on her!"

She reaches out and places her hand on my upper arm. "Calm down. She'll be fine. She has a driver with her and will be home soon."

"Ms. Evans! Ember can't just leave the house and walk around. It's New York! Are you crazy?"

"You can't keep her locked in a gilded cage, Christopher. She needs to explore and learn to grow. I understand your need to protect her, but you're hurting her by keeping her locked away in this house with no one but me as her company. I'm watching the poor girl fall into depression. It's not healthy, and you know it. She needs to get out, meet people, and be active in day-to-day life. She also doesn't want to disappoint you, Christopher. So I think she's not being completely open and honest with you. And she's trying hard with your mother. I can see she wants her approval so badly."

"No one gets my mother's approval," I snap. "I'll inform Ember on this. But still... Ms. Evans... she can't leave the house! It's not safe."

"She needs to be let out of the cage." The woman refuses to back down, and it infuriates me.

"I trusted you to watch over her!" I boom, turning to storm out of the house and hunt her down.

"I don't need a babysitter," I hear Ember's voice say as she enters the living room. "I was perfectly fine and am now home safe." She motions to her body to indicate she's all intact and smiles. "As you can see. I'm here in one piece."

I rush to her side and take her into my arms, grateful to see her back. "Jesus. Why did you leave? If you wanted to go there, all you had to do was ask, and I would have taken you."

"It was fine. I had a really nice time, actually. I went to see the *Alice in Wonderland* statue, spoke to a nice gentleman—"

"Who?" I interrupt, breaking my hold of her to stare at her eyes. "You can't just go talking to strangers. It could be a reporter or... you can't just talk to complete strangers." I turn to glare at Ms. Evans. "See? This is why she needs to be with me.

She doesn't understand the way people act yet. She could get chewed up and spit out."

Ember takes the step that separates us and goes on tiptoe so she can kiss my forehead. "You'll get permanent wrinkles if you keep furrowing your brow like this. Stop being angry at Ms. Evans. She was right in helping me. I needed to get out and explore a little, and no harm came of it. And you can't always be with me, Christopher. I needed to get out, and nothing bad came of it. So calm down." She briefly pecks my lips and winks at Ms. Evans. "Thank you for the suggestion. It was fun. I want to go back when I have more time to really explore the entire park. I only had time to take a short walk."

"With me next time," I say, glaring at Ms. Evans and then at Ember. I can tell I've lost this battle and being angry isn't going to get me anywhere, but I still want my wishes known.

Ember giggles and nods. "Whatever you say, husband. Whatever you say."

I can tell she's mocking me, but I have to admit I like it. She does seem refreshed and happy. Yes, I want her safe... but more than anything, I want her happy.

14

EMBER

I'M HAPPY TO SEE CHRISTOPHER GETTING BACK TO work, but a selfish part of me doesn't like it when he leaves, especially after the awful dinner I had with Louisa the other night. Luckily, I hadn't seen her since, so I'm doing my best to act as if nothing happened. I don't want to tell Christopher about the dinner, because I don't want to upset him. I believe it's best to just ignore and move on. The woman needs time to adjust.

Papa Rich used to tell me that an injured animal is dangerous. Pain can make even the nicest creature vicious. And that is exactly what Louisa Davenport is. Hurt. I can understand that. She missed a milestone of her son's life. Hurt has made her mean to me. I have to rise above that. I have to.

But I do miss Christopher. There have been long days where he's gone from the time we wake up until after I've already fallen asleep. He's in demand now since the interview. His "fame" has helped his career even more, and he's getting freelance offers that he's struggling to turn down. People want him to travel all over the world, and when I tell him to take the opportunity, he brushes off the idea. He tells me that he doesn't want to leave me for so long and doesn't feel I'm ready for international travel.

He's probably right.

I'm adjusting, but not well. The sounds of the city are loud, and the constant movement has me jittery. Taking a simple walk gives me anxiety, and though I try to hide the feelings from Christopher, I know he sees it. He feels it.

And then there's Papa Rich.

I know he's alive. I can feel it in my bones.

Christopher tells me over and over again that even if he's alive, he can't hurt us again. He can't reach us.

I don't believe him.

He doesn't know Papa Rich like I do, and even though I'm practically locked away in Louisa's tower like Rapunzel, Papa Rich will find a way to reach me. It's just a matter of time.

"It's one night," Christopher says as he throws some clothes in a small black suitcase. "The shoot is in LA, and I can't make it a turnaround trip like I want to. One night, and I'll be home."

I don't know if he's telling me this to make me feel better, or for him to feel better about leaving me.

"And my mother is here. And she's having the party tonight that will be fun for you to attend and keep you busy. Louisa Davenport is known for her social gatherings with all the glitz, fantastic food, and expensive wines."

"Are Christina and Michael coming?" I ask, hating the idea of attending a party without Christopher. I sit cross-legged on the bed, watching his every move.

He chuckles as he folds a shirt. "They aren't exactly in her social circle."

"Maybe I should just stay upstairs and read," I offer.

He pauses, looks at me, and then smiles. "Make an appearance, let everyone see how beautiful Louisa Davenport's daughter-in-law is, and enjoy a bite to eat. If you're having an awful time after that, then feel free to excuse yourself. But I think it will be good for you to interact with some new people and keep your mind off me being gone."

"I suppose you're right," I agree as I fiddle with the hem of my skirt between my fingers. "But with all the people coming, will we all be... safe?"

"The media won't be allowed inside. Don't worry; my mother still has security outside the house. If anything, it will add to the elite and exclusive element of her party. I'm sure she simply loves it."

I'm not referring to the media, but I don't tell him that I actually meant if we'll be safe from Papa Rich. He could walk into the party undetected if there's a constant flow of people entering and exiting the house. The FBI team assigned to the case officially announced Richard as a wanted man. They are also searching for Scarecrow, as they haven't been able to locate him either. They found Scarecrow's old mining camp they believe he was living in, but it had been vacated. Their assumption is that Richard and Scarecrow are on the run together. They've ruled me out as an accomplice, or at least that's what Christopher's team of lawyers have told us.

Every time I bring up Papa Rich to Christopher, I can see it annoys him. Each time, he is getting a little more short with me and a little more impatient. I hate keeping things from my husband, but at the same time, maybe he's right. Maybe I'm being paranoid over nothing. Maybe I need to set that ghost haunting me free.

Maybe Papa Rich died in that fire.

Or at the very least, maybe that fire and our escape really will be the last I'll see of him regardless of if he escaped or not. I know I can't heal until I stop thinking about him. I know that.

Christopher is trying to convince me to see a therapist to help me work through my feelings, but I don't want to speak to a stranger. At least not yet. I know it's not good that I really don't want to leave our bedroom. I feel safe in it. I feel secure. Every strange face that looks at me reminds me of a bee sting.

It was bad enough that I had to go to a doctor to be examined and to get vaccinations that I never had growing up. Christopher also convinced me it would be best to be put on birth control. I want a baby but have to agree that I don't want one quite yet. I didn't realize that it was so easy to prevent one from coming. But the experience at the doctor's office was awful. They asked so many personal questions, and I felt like I was a science project to them. I hated it, and I vowed to stay healthy so I never have to return… or at least until my next round of awful vaccines.

"I'm going to miss you," I confess as I watch him zip up his suitcase.

He leans forward and kisses me on the lips. "I'm going to miss you, too." He pulls away, runs his fingers through my hair, and adds, "I'll be back tomorrow night. Try to have some fun while I'm gone. I'm also just a phone call away."

Christopher gave me a cell phone when he started work again. I hate using it and keeping it on me at all times as he asked me to do. I feel so incompetent and inept in using it. I also don't like talking into something to hear my husband's voice. It feels unnatural and actually only makes me miss him more.

We walk down the stairs to the foyer hand in hand, something Louisa clearly hates when she sees us. Her eyes dart to our intertwined fingers, and if the daggers shooting from her heavy-lashed eyes could slice each finger off my hand, she would have.

"Are you sure you have to go?" she asks Christopher. "I was so hoping for you to be at tonight's party. So many people want to see you and talk to you. Everyone had been absolutely devastated at your funeral."

"I'm sure there will be many more parties," Christopher says as he puts down his suitcase and gives his mother a hug. "Ember will be there for the both of us."

"Alone? Do you feel that Amber should be alone?"

"Ember," I correct. I hate when she calls me Amber, which she now does every single time.

"Your name is Amber, dear. Amber Jennings. Remember?"

She's talking to me like I'm a child. She almost has a singsong tone to each syllable, and I want to scream at her. *My name is Ember. Ember!*

"Mom, we discussed this. Ember prefers the name she's always known."

"But her legal name is Amber."

"Mom," Cristopher warns. "As I was saying, Ember will love meeting your friends in my spot."

Louisa shoots another glare my way. "Are you sure that's a good idea? There will be a lot of people there and—"

"She'll be fine," he says as he walks over to me and quickly pecks my lips, and then adds, "I'll see you tomorrow night." He picks up his suitcase and walks out the door before calling out, "You ladies have fun tonight. But don't have too much without me."

When the door closes, Louisa turns her attention on me. "It's semi-formal tonight. If you plan on attending, make sure you are dressed accordingly." She points at my ballet shoes I've slowly gotten used to wearing. "*Those* will not do. You really should get some heels like a proper lady."

I usually feel a sense of shame every time Louisa points out something she finds wrong about me, but not in regards to the shoes. They were from a friend's store, and I'm proud of them. "Christina told me these shoes are very in style." I notice my voice is haughty, and although foreign, I feel it's appropriate to have toward this woman.

"Who? Christina? She has that boho shop I wouldn't be caught dead in." Louisa looks as if she's smelling something foul, but then she notices the catering department is not setting up a table to her specifications and runs toward them, barking orders before I can defend my friend.

I want Christopher's mother to like me, but it may be an impossible task.

Glad I have several dresses that are far fancier than the ones I've been wearing daily, I go upstairs to start getting ready for the party. I know it's important to Christopher that I go, and although I'd much prefer not to ... I do have something to prove to Louisa. I'm not the poor girl who haunted the schoolhouse anymore. I'm not the victim of a madman.

I'm not Amber Jennings.

I'm Ember. Ember *Davenport*.

A Davenport. Mrs. Christopher Davenport.

15

ALL DAY, I MENTALLY PREPARED. I TOOK A LONG bath. I read a new book. I focused on what I want out of the future—but more specifically, tonight. I thought of Christopher and how he clearly had faith in me before he left. And I spent some time thinking of Papa Rich. Not in a fond way, or a scared way, but in a way I believe is helping me heal. I realize I have to accept the fact that he truly is a bad man. What he did to me was bad. His acts were not out of love but rather from sickness.

I spent today trying to heal and become strong. And for the first time since arriving in this house, I started to feel like I was getting used to things.

Accepting.

I'm proud of myself and actually excited for the party. Standing in front of the full-length mirror, I know I've managed to pull off the semi-formal that Louisa wants for her event. Thanks to Christina thinking ahead and making me get a rose-colored satin dress with a dipping neckline I first thought too sexy, I'm happy I listened to her. I've also managed to pull my hair up into a twist, showing off my neck and shoulders, which is also something I'm not used to. I think Christopher would love seeing me like this.

I'm different.

I'm no longer the scared woman locked in a cellar, jumping at the slightest sound.

Right now, this very second, I see a reflection of confidence. I can be the brave woman society demands. I can be the woman Christopher deserves by his side. I can be her. I can.

The sound of guests already arriving downstairs doesn't scare me. It should... or at least it would... but not right now. Instead, I'm beautiful, and I know I can go down there and be charming. I can meet people as Mrs. Davenport. The younger and prettier Mrs. Davenport.

I laugh out loud at my thoughts and imagine what Louisa would think if she could hear them.

Still wearing flats—because it's all I own—I walk to the bedroom door. I don't care what Louisa says. I think they're pretty, and I'm going to believe what Christina says—that I'm in style. When I go to open the door, I can't.

It's stuck.

I jiggle the handle, trying to force the door open, but nothing I do is working.

Is it stuck? Or is it locked?

Who would lock the door?

I was in the bath for a long time and wouldn't hear the click....

No.

Who would purposely lock my door?

I knock on the door and call out, "Hello? Can anyone hear me? Hello?"

There's laughter and music downstairs, and I know no one can hear me from there, but maybe Louisa is upstairs, or Ms. Evans. I jiggle the handle harder this time, feeling a sense of panic. I don't like feeling... trapped. Locked away. Helpless and unable to flee.

It's just like the cellar.

It's just like the cellar!

I can scream; maybe I will be heard then. But I don't want to make a scene. I don't want to embarrass Christopher. What if it's just as simple as the door being stuck, and I overreact over nothing? They all already see me as fragile. I want to be strong and brave. I'm in the rose dress that gives me courage.

"Hello? Can anyone help? The door is stuck."

Nothing.

I walk over to the window and look down at the people below. I see guests dressed in gowns, furs, and suits entering the house. It's a blur of faces, and I blink away the building fear that something is wrong. Why am I locked in the room? Is someone coming?

Is Papa Rich coming for me?

Does he know Christopher's gone for the night, Louisa is preoccupied, and the security is distracted by all the people? He's smart. He could be watching. Planning. He could have known about this party days ago when the invitations went out. Maybe he's been watching Christopher's every move and has learned his schedule, even as chaotic and unreliable as it is.

Maybe I can bang on the window and the people down below will see me.

But as I get ready to pound on the glass, I pause. If they see me looking out the window, wide-eyed and in need... I will forever be the ghost looking out the window of the schoolhouse. I will never be free. That's how they will see me. That's who I will be.

Deciding to try one more time, I go back to the door and shake harder than before. I even throw my weight against the wood, hoping I can free it. The laughter and blending of voices on the other side taunt me with where I should be.

Maybe Louisa will notice I'm missing and come up looking for me.

I smirk and walk to my bed. Who am I kidding? The woman is grateful I'm not down there. She's probably pleased thinking I got too scared or worked up to attend. Instead, I'm holed up in my room, hiding out. Yeah... she won't come looking for me at all.

Looking at the cell phone on the side table, I consider calling Christopher. I don't know his mother's number or Ms. Evans's. Maybe he does and can call them to have them let me out of the room. But I know he's on a shoot, and I don't want to bother him with something as embarrassing as being locked in my room somehow. I definitely don't want to tell him I'm afraid Papa Rich could be part of it, as I'm pushing my luck already with my "irrational" fear. I don't want to be that wife. The crazy wife who calls in a panic.

Whatever. I didn't even want to go to the party to begin with.

But then, I did.

I do.

I've always had to watch from afar all my life. Families smiling. People laughing while having a fun day out. I was a spy on their time, and as I sit in the room on the edge of my bed, hearing the excited energy below, I'm still the same freak from Hallelujah Junction. I can hear them having a good time without me. I can listen on and do nothing, just as I had to watch from the schoolhouse without being able to be part of the crowds.

Feeling sorry for myself, I pull back the comforter of the bed to crawl in and try to forget this night all together. And then I see it.

I blink away the madness, but it remains rooted in place.

Straw.

There's straw in my bed.

They were here. Scarecrow. Papa Rich.

I know they were here.

It's their way of saying hello.

My eyes dart around the room as if I'm going to find them standing right before me. Oh my God. They've come for me. I knew they would. I knew it.

I bolt off the bed and run to the bathroom, needing to confirm they aren't inside waiting for me. Seeing the empty room doesn't make me feel better. It just means they are toying with me as my cat Pine Cone would toy with a field mouse that snuck in the house. I inhale deeply to see if I can smell onion and body odor but smell nothing. Yet...

Yet...

Yet...

They're here. They. Are. Here.

I run to the door and begin banging hard against it. I don't care if the guests hear me now. I don't care if I embarrass myself and Louisa. I need the safety in numbers. I can't just sit in this room and wait for them to come. I know they are waiting. They are waiting until the perfect time to kidnap me and take me with them. I know it! I feel it!

"Help! I'm stuck in here! Get me out! Help!" I start throwing my shoulder and full body weight at the door but only feel the hard and unforgiving door slapping me back.

No one is coming. The party is loud. The fun is overpowering. No one has time for a scared, crazy woman upstairs.

I sprint to the large walk-in closet and slam the door behind me. I see a lock and make sure I'm in control on this one. I'm locking myself inside. Sitting in the farthest corner, I pull my knees up to my chest and close my eyes. I try not to picture Hallelujah Junction. I try to force the visions of Scarecrow in my bedroom out of my mind. I try not to hear Papa Rich telling me I've been a bad, bad girl and must be punished. I can hear the sound of the leather lash against my bare ass. I can feel the sting on memory alone. I'm going to pay for burning our home. He's going to make sure of it. I know he will.

I notice that near one of Christopher's shoes is another piece of straw.

Scarecrow was in our closet. Was he hiding in here? For how long? Watching?

I cry out but cover my mouth instantly as I do. I don't want them to find me. If they walk into the bedroom, I want them to think I'm at the party.

Don't find me.

Don't find me.

Don't find me.

Looking at the locked door, I realize I left the cell phone by the bed. Should I go get it? And then what?

I can't call Christopher. What can he do? He's in LA and hours and hours away from me even if he did rush back.

I can't call the police. What will I say? Tell them I found straw in my bed and closet? They'd all think I finally lost my mind. The poor kidnapped girl finally broke.

Stretching out my hand, I take hold of the straw. I need to feel it between my fingers to make sure this isn't all in my head. I smell it but only smell straw. It doesn't reek, but did Scarecrow's straw ever smell?

This is all wrong. I should have never let Christopher convince me to escape. We were happy. We were. I could have been a good wife there. I would have worked every single day to please him. Chained or not, at least we would have been safe.

But now...

We've angered Papa Rich.

I've seen over and over what happens when you anger Papa Rich. There may not be the Old Mill anymore with the acid pits, but he'll find a new way to make us suffer. He won't let Christopher get away with what he did. Christopher stole his daughter, and there will be a brutal and agonizing price for that. He'll make me watch as he tortures the man I love. Just like he made me watch as he killed all those trespassers.

So many screams.

So many howls of misery.

And just like all those times before, there is nothing I can do to stop it. There's not Hallelujah Junction to return to and beg for forgiveness. Everything is gone. Nothing but ash. Nothing but the ghosts of all the dead. Nothing.

"Ember?" I hear called out from the other side of the door.

I freeze and look around for a weapon to use, but there's nothing but shoes and clothes.

"Ember? Are you in here?"

I recognize the voice. It's Louisa. She's here.

"In here," I cry out, wondering if it's all in my head. "In here."

My heart stops in anticipation. I'm frozen in place to see if what I hear is real or just wishful delusion.

The door to the closet tries to open, but the lock I used keeps it closed. I lunge for the door to unlock it but pause before I do. "Louisa? Is that you?"

"Yes."

Unlocking the door, I open it wide, anxious to be free of my prison. When I do, I see Louisa and three other women standing behind her. Each woman has her mouth open and eyes wide. One of them even gasps when she sees me.

Louisa puts her hand to her heart and takes a stunned step backward. "What in the world are you doing locked in the closet?"

"I..." I can see everyone is afraid of me. They aren't moving enough for me to exit the closet, so I stay in place. "I was locked in the bedroom. I couldn't get out no matter how hard I tried. I think Papa Rich did it. I think he's here. So I was hiding. He's here." My body starts to shake as I say the words. "He's here."

"What are you talking about?" Louisa asks, her eyes changing from a look of shock to a look of detest. "The door wasn't locked. We just walked in here perfectly fine."

"No. It was locked. I even called out for help, but—"

Louisa turns her head to look at her friends who have yet to stop staring at me as if I'm some sort of two-headed circus freak. "I'm sorry you ladies have to witness this. Ember has... been through a lot."

Their looks of shock morph to looks of pity. I hate these looks even more.

"You poor thing," one woman says.

"You're safe now," another adds.

"You don't understand," I say as I reach for Louisa's hand. She pulls away as if touching me would cause a chemical reaction to her creamy white skin. I pause when I realize these women—including Louisa—think I've gone mad.

"You need help, Ember," Louisa says, glancing at her friends for their agreement. The other three women nod as if they know who I am and are in a place to know what's best for me. "I've been telling Christopher this over and over again." She pulls out her phone from a small clutch she has around her wrist and begins dialing.

"Louisa, I'm not making this up. This isn't in my head. If you will just sit down and listen to me, you'll see we are all in danger. Papa Rich is a vengeful man, and he's going to punish us all for our misdeeds." I hand her the piece of straw. "This is proof that Scarecrow is here with him. He left it behind to mess with me, to mess with us all."

The other women all step away at this time. The movement allows me to leave the closet and enter the room, which only makes them cower farther away. They're all acting like I'm going to hurt them.

Realizing these women are terrified of me, I retreat back into the closet to give them all some space.

To give me some space.

I can't breathe. I can't think. I can't process.

All I know is no one is listening, and we're all in danger.

"Come home now," Louisa says into the phone as she shoots daggers from her eyes at me. "It's Ember. She's lost her mind completely. You need to come home and deal with this immediately."

I open my mouth to tell her she's wrong. I'm saner and more levelheaded than I've been since arriving. I'm finally seeing what's going to happen. I'm no longer hiding from truth. He's coming. He's coming.

"Christopher! I'm telling you to come home."

16

CHRISTOPHER

It was time to face the demon head-on.

Maybe not the smartest choice, considering that my mind wasn't in the game for this photo shoot, but still, something had to be done. I took the opportunity of being alone—without Ember—on the plane to finally read all the information that had been gathered on Richard by my attorneys and Jason. I spent the last few weeks trying to get the thought of Richard out of Ember's mind, which meant not discussing him, not bringing up the investigation, and trying to forget this awful experience ever occurred. Ember needs to move on, and the only way I feel she can do so is by trying to erase Papa Rich from her memories and future thoughts.

But now that I'm alone for a longer stretch of time, it's time I see what the current status is.

Snapping picture after picture of the latest starlet, I try to focus on her, but all I can see are the beady and evil eyes of Richard. Reading the file fucked me up. What little healing I had done had just been ripped wide open and is now an oozing, festering wound again.

Richard is now referred as The Ghost Town Killer and officially considered a serial killer. Twenty-two victims turned up missing in Hallelujah Junction and are now presumed dead per the accounts Ember was able to give the authorities. They believe The Ghost Town Killer is now responsible for all of their deaths. The information in my files reveals that not a single body was able to be exhumed from the acid pits due to the conditions. It truly was a genius move for a serial killer to use the acid pits as his mode for murder. No evidence left behind. Only two witnesses.

Me and Ember.

I saw a picture of the couple who tried to help Ember and me, which cost them their lives. It was like a punch to the gut repeatedly, and I can't help but feel like blood is on my hands. They died because of me. I put them in the situation, and I was helpless in saving them. But they were only two of the twenty-two victims. Which means poor Ember has twenty more deaths to feel guilty over than I do.

I can't imagine what that must do to her.

I know what two gruesome deaths is doing to me.

I have nightmares with their faces in them. I hear their screams still. I still remember the look in their eyes right before they were pushed to their deaths. I'm not sure I'll ever be able to forget.

The media is loving the story of The Schoolhouse Ghost and The *Rolling Stone* Photographer. Articles calling us a twisted and perverse love story.

A demented love affair.

In the file, Jason included official offers for book and movie deals I just briefly skimmed over. The last thing I want is to see our ordeal on the big screen. Who the fuck would they get to play me? I actually chuckled on the plane at the very thought.

Reading it on the plane had been surreal. It's hard to believe I not only lived it but survived it. But the hardest part isn't what happened—it's dealing with it all now. Yes, I got my career back, and yes, I'm a free man, but I often feel trapped. My breathing restricts often as my soul feels shredded with what occurred. I try to be strong for Ember, and yet, I sometimes wonder if she's far stronger than I am.

Or maybe we're both just fucked.

Fortunately for me and my model, my years of experience allow me to operate on autopilot, and I'm somehow able to finish the shoot and get some excellent photos that will work for what I need. I'm also happy the crew mostly leaves me alone during the shoot. I think word has spread that I'm not open to discussing the kidnapping and it's best to check your curiosity at the door if you want to work with me currently and for any future gigs. I've never been one to be a diva, but if that's the rumor, then good. They are correct.

I don't want to talk about shit.

Leave me the fuck alone if you just want to be a rubbernecker and be around the *Rolling Stone* Photographer married to The Schoolhouse Ghost. Move the fuck along.

As I'm packing up the last of my gear, I hear a familiar voice from behind me. "Hi, Christopher."

Looking over my shoulder, I see Marissa standing a few feet away with a warm smile but nervous hands fiddling in front of her stomach.

"Marissa?" I stand up from the crouching position I'm in. "What are you doing here?"

"I still have friends at *Rolling Stone*. I found out you were coming to LA on business, and well—" She repositions her weight from one foot to the other. "—I wanted a chance to speak to you alone. We need to talk."

I haven't seen or spoken to Marissa since the first day I returned home, and although I was hoping to avoid this conversation all together, I also know she deserves closure. I should have called her and explained long ago. It was selfish of me not to.

"Can we go get a drink?" she asks. "If you're all done."

"I'd like that," I say, glancing down at my phone to make sure I didn't get any calls while I was doing the shoot. "Does Mickey's sound good?"

"I was hoping you'd say that." Her face lights up. "It's our favorite whenever we come to LA."

She's not talking in past tense, and I wish she would. It *was* our favorite. *Was.*

We both don't say much until we're sitting in our usual booth and have ordered our usual drinks and our favorite potato skins as a snack. Guilt runs through my veins at how routine and natural it feels, and a big part of me misses the normal of it all. There was a day that I never thought I'd be back to doing these kinds of things again.

I decide to be the first to speak. "I'm sorry I haven't reached out to you."

Her eyes lower to her drink, and she nods slowly. "I was hoping you would. I kept waiting. I wanted to give you space and time, but... I kept waiting."

"I don't know if I'll ever have enough time, to be honest." I take a drink of my beer and reach for a skin. "I don't ever think I'll be the man I once was."

"I watched you and Ember in that interview. It was hard hearing what happened to you. Even harder seeing you with her."

"I'm sorry."

"What about me, Christopher? Was I not your girlfriend before all this?"

"You were. Yes. But everything changed the minute that chain was forced around my ankle."

"Why? Why do your feelings for me have to change? You and I had something really special. We still do."

"Everything changed. I changed," I admit. "I tried to fight it every step of the way. I tried to resist. But sadly, your and my relationship was collateral damage."

"Did you resist *her*? Why did you marry her?"

"I was forced to. It was the reason I wasn't killed by Richard to begin with. He wanted me to marry his daughter, and that was the only way to survive. I was living one day at a time and trying to figure out a way to get out of there."

"Okay... I get that. But then why stay with her now? You aren't *forced* to be with her now to survive."

I sit back and release a rush of air from my lungs. I don't know how honest to be with her. I don't want to hurt her any more than I have to, but I also know if I'm truly honest, the words will sting like a son of a bitch.

"You're home," she adds. "I'm here, and I can be here for you while you recover."

"I'm married, Marissa," I state firmly. "I know you and others don't think I'm really married, considering how it was done and the legalities of it, but I made more than one vow to Ember. Something happened while we were locked up together. A bond and connection I've never had with anyone else. I'm sorry, as I know this has to be tough to hear. We both lived through something I can never explain, because there are no real words. I see her as my wife, just as she sees me as her husband."

"But do you love her?"

I reach for my beer as I consider the question. "I do." I look up at her and see tears wetting her eyes. "I know it's hard to believe. But I do. Trust me, I didn't think it was possible, and at the beginning, I was playing along so I could try to escape. But things changed. We changed while there. And yes, I do love Ember." I pause, taking a drink so I can wash away the words I know just destroyed the woman in front of me. "I'm sorry, Marissa. I truly am."

"I don't believe you. Or maybe you *think* you love her. But I think you feel a sense of responsibility for her. I think you know she has no one but you, so you feel guilty. I think you may be suffering from survivor's guilt or PTSD or something. But I don't think you truly love her."

I nodded. "I'm sure you're right in the fact that I'm suffering from all that. And yes, I do feel a sense of responsibility for her. I have an almost primal need to protect her. But that doesn't change the fact that

I do love her, and I have no intention of ending the marriage with her."

She wipes at a falling tear. "Did you ever love me?"

"I did. But I'm not the same man anymore. Maybe I'm worse off, maybe better in some ways. Regardless, I'm not the same man."

"Your mother told me that Ember is crazy. Certifiably insane. She told me that you feel like you have to protect her. That you feel responsible. Could you be mistaking that as love?"

"She's not crazy," I snap. "Maybe broken, but then so am I. My mother has no idea. No one does. Until you face death head-on and worry if you're going to live another day, no one can judge us."

"It's not just your mother talking. Christopher, you look crazy too. You brought home this waif of a woman who is batshit crazy, and you're calling her your wife. And then you go on national television announcing it to all. I think you're fucked in the head." She pauses and swallows hard. "Which I understand after what you went through. But I'm here to try to talk some reason into you."

"She's my wife. She is. I'm sorry, but nothing you, my mother, or anyone else can say will change that."

"You always told me that what you liked about me was my independence. You liked that I didn't have to be rescued or taken care of. And yet, now you brought home a stray who needs you. *Needs* you." Her voice is rising, and I can see the pain on her face is quickly being replaced by anger.

I reach across the table to pat her hand, which she pulls away from as if I just burned her. "I know I hurt you. I know this isn't what you wanted to hear when you flew across the country. But it's the truth."

Marissa reaches for a napkin and starts dabbing at her eyes, careful not to smear her makeup. "I feel like you're self-destructing, and I'm watching you die right in front of me. This isn't you, Christopher. This isn't you."

"I agree with you that the Christopher who was your boyfriend months ago is not me. I agree."

"Let me stay with you tonight." When I open my mouth to object, she quickly adds, "One night. Just for you to see what it's like to be with me again. To remind you of what we had. Maybe so we can find that man you lost again. I think he's still in there. I believe you still love me. Let me show you. Can you at least give me that? One night?"

"Marissa—"

"One night. It's all I ask. You owe me that. At the very least to give me closure. I'm a victim in this too. Help me just like you help Ember." The tears are flowing down her face now, and no amount of dabbing is preventing the running of mascara. "If after tonight you still want to be with Ember, then I'll walk away gracefully."

My phone rings just as I get ready to respond. I glance down and see it's my mother calling. "I need to get this," I say, answering the phone before Marissa can object. "Mom? Everything okay? How's the party?"

"Come home now," she says firmly.

"What? Why?"

"It's Ember. She's lost her mind completely. You need to come home and deal with this immediately."

"Is she okay? Is she there with you? Let me talk to her."

"Christopher! I'm telling you to come home."

17

CHRISTOPHER

"WHERE IS SHE?" I DEMAND AS I STORM INTO THE house.

The flight across the country I managed to book the minute my mother called demanding I return home had me nearly exploding. Hours of feeling helpless, knowing Ember needed me and there was absolutely nothing I could do until I got back to New York. But now I'm home, and I need to find Ember and be with her immediately.

Ms. Evans is standing on the bottom stair with a tray in her hand. "I was just going to bring her up some food and drink."

My mother walks in from the living room, which still has signs of her party hours ago that the catering company hasn't collected. "She's hiding in the closet upstairs. She's completely lost her mind. I've never been so embarrassed in all my life. Veronica, Michelle, and Diana all witnessed it and left here simply mortified. It was awful, Christopher. Awful!"

"Why the fuck is she in the closet?"

My words appear to slap my mother, because she gasps before screeching, "How would I know? When she didn't come down for the party, my friends and I went upstairs to check on her. We entered her room to find Ember locked in her closet. After calling out several times, she finally opened the door with her hair wild, her eyes bulging— Frankly, she looked as if she were on drugs. Then she started rambling about how Papa Rich was in the house and going to get her. She locked herself inside to hide from him. She told my friends they were in danger. I swear, Christopher, I may never live this down. I can't imagine what those women are saying about me now. Ember purposely scared them."

"Why would she think that Richard was in the house? Did something happen to spook her?"

"I went to check on her and if she needed anything," Ms. Evans chimes in. "And she spoke about there being straw in her bed and closet. But I didn't see any straw. I searched everywhere, but there wasn't any."

"Of course there was no straw!" Louisa snapped. "Ramblings of a madwoman. I can't have this going on in my house. She's unstable!"

"Mom, calm down. Ember's just going through a lot right now. Assimilating into this world, with the media, all the attention, and just.... Cut the girl some slack, will ya? She's not doing anything intentionally to upset you or your friends. She's scared."

"She needs help! Serious, professional help."

I nod in agreement. "And I'll get her some. You're right. Getting an expert to try to help her make sense of all this could be a good thing." I pause and then ask, "What about security? Did they see anything out of the ordinary?"

"Of course they didn't," my mother snaps. "There was nothing to see. You don't honestly think a one-legged man hobbled into my house, followed by one of the most wanted men on the FBI list right now, undetected? The girl has lost her mind. She's mental. I don't blame her for being mental, but the fact is that we are not equipped to deal with her.

You can't make this woman your problem anymore. You deserve better."

"Mother," I warn, trying to be patient, considering Ember did frazzle the hell out of her. "I know you're upset. I'm sorry, and I'll handle it."

Ms. Evans holds up the tray. "She hasn't eaten or had anything to drink, and I was going to see if I could get something in her."

I take hold of the tray and start walking upstairs. "I'll do it, thank you."

I don't know what to think about everything. I shouldn't have left her. It was too soon. She snapped, because she wasn't ready for me to be away. I should have known better than to suggest she attend a party and then leave as if she's ready to deal with normal life so casually. This is my fault.

"Ember?" I call out as I enter the room, placing the tray on the desk. "It's Christopher."

I walk to the closet, and my heart breaks when I open it. She's sitting in a ball in the farthest corner with bloodshot eyes.

"I'm so sorry, Christopher," she begins on a sob. "I'm so sorry. I don't know what's going on anymore. I feel so.... I don't know what I feel."

I rush to her side and take her into my arms. "What happened? Why are you in the closet?"

"I was so afraid, and... I scared those women. I scared your mother. I made a fool of myself."

"Why are you afraid? Did something happen?" I begin stroking her hair and placing small kisses on her forehead as I hold her firmly against my body.

"It doesn't matter anymore," she mumbles into my chest and then begins crying harder.

"It matters to me."

She raises her eyes to me, and her lip quivers. "I'm always going to be the freak. I'm always going to be the girl who people stare at and talk about behind her back. And it's my fault. Mine. Those women saw me tonight and are going to walk away telling everyone they witnessed the crazy ghost girl they saw on the news. I'm living up to all the rumors. I had a chance to be normal tonight, and instead... this happens." She sobs harder than I've ever seen. Her fists dig into her eyes as she tries to wipe away the tears.

"It's all right. I'm here." I scoop my arm under her legs and pick her up. I carry her to the bed and place her gently on it, repositioning us so I can hold her in my arms again. I may never let her go.

"I saw straw—Scarecrow's straw—but then Ms. Evans said there was no straw. And... I thought they were here. I really thought they were here. I really thought I saw straw."

"You're safe," I soothe. "There's no one here."

Ember pulls away, wipes at her eyes, and stares up at me. "I don't think we are. I think Papa Rich is never going to give up on me. On us. We wronged him, and he's a man with conviction to right any wrong."

Frustration bubbles inside me, and though a part of me wants to shout and scream at Ember for once again letting that man control our thoughts, I know she's in a fragile state and I need to be calm. I also agree with my mother. Ember does need help. We both do. We need someone to help us navigate these fears and emotions of hers. She's afraid, and I'm pissed. I can't be sympathetic like she needs, and she can't handle the rage inside me.

"You need to stop calling him Papa Rich," I say as calmly as I can, but I know the words come out harsh. "He's not your father. He's not in our lives anymore and never will be again. I told you I'd protect you, and I mean it. He can't kidnap you again. It will never happen."

"I tried," she says softly as she rests her cheek on my chest again. "I really tried. I got all dressed up, did my hair, and was actually really excited to go to the party. But then I got locked inside, I swear I saw straw, and... I freaked out. Maybe I'm going crazy. Maybe I've always been that way."

"Anxiety can do that," I say. "Maybe you had a panic attack or something to cause this. I'm sorry. I left you too soon and pushed you too hard to live life like nothing happened to us. I think this was just your mind and body telling you that you aren't ready yet. And that's okay. We don't have to rush things. There's no timetable. We go at our own speed."

"I'm not sure I'll ever get used to this. I feel like I'm in a storm and, no matter what I do, I can't find shelter," she confesses.

"I know. I'm in that storm with you as well, but we will find shelter. I'm going to find us a therapist to help guide us in all this. Will that be okay?"

She tenses but then eventually nods. "Okay."

"I love you, Ember. Just hold on to that one fact when you feel lost. I love you."

There's a long moment of silence, and then she says, "Your mother hates me. I don't blame her."

She sniffles, but it sounds as if she's at least done sobbing.

"She'll get over what happened. She's embarrassed. That's all, and you aren't the first person to have a scene at one of her parties. Trust me, she's witnessed far worse."

"I'm sorry. I really am. I'm also sorry you had to fly back so soon. I hope I didn't hurt anything with your work."

I sigh and pull her off me. "Work's fine. It's been a really long day for the both of us. It's late, and we could both use some rest. Let's get undressed and go to bed."

I'm pretty sure the minute my head hits the pillow, I will be out in seconds. The adrenaline is wearing off now that I know Ember is safe and by my side.

When we both crawl into bed to sleep, Ember curls her body up next to mine. I have a flashback of when we first slept together in the dank cellar with nothing but a couple of blankets to keep us warm.

"I'll try to do better," she murmurs as sleep is setting in for both of us.

"You're trying your best. I know you are." I close my eyes, no longer able to keep them open. "We'll figure it out," I say with a yawn. "We always have up until this point and will continue to do so."

I hear her breathing deepen, and I know she's off to sleep. I just hope she doesn't have any more nightmares. I hope the same for me.

Fuck you, Richard.

Fuck you straight to hell.

Part of me hopes he dares show his face here. I'd make him pay for everything he did to this woman. He's broken her, but I will make sure I pick up all the pieces and help her figure out how to heal.

Come, motherfucker.

Come to my house.

I'm ready for you.

18

CHRISTOPHER

FRUSTRATION IS NOT SOMETHING I HANDLE WELL. Patience is not a quality I possess. Hanging up the phone with my real estate agent has me wanting to throw something at my editor's door. The only thing keeping me from doing so is that I'm borrowing his office after a shoot to have a little alone time, and trashing his office won't go over well.

"The market is crazy right now," he said.

"I'm working as hard as I can," he assured.

"I found a fixer upper, but it's not ready to move in to," he offered.

"Maybe in a few months, more inventory will open up," he ended the conversation with.

Ember and I need to get out of my mother's house before she truly drives both of us crazy. I can feel Ember is growing frustrated herself. She doesn't understand why we're in this holding pattern, and I know she's as anxious as I am to get in our own house that she can finally make her home. Transition into normal society isn't being helped by her walking the halls of my mother's elegant and stuffy estate, unable to call anything hers.

There's a knock on the door, and I figure it's Max wanting his office back. "Come in, I'm done," I call out, trying to shake off my annoyance at not having the call with my agent that I wanted.

"Max said I could find you here," Marissa says as she enters the office and closes the door behind her.

Fuck. She's not going to just let this be.

"I know I may not be the person you want to see," she begins as she walks fully into the room. "But you left so abruptly in LA that we weren't able to finish our conversation."

"I felt we did," I state, not wanting to be mean but still having to be honest.

"I spoke to your mother last night, and she told me that Ember is having a really hard time. That you both are considering having her get professional help. At an institute. I'm here to offer my support in any way. I know how hard this must be, and I want to be here for you."

I let out a breath at the same level and intensity a dragon would release a flame. "No. I'm not having my wife committed. It's never been an option, nor will it. This is nothing more than the ramblings of a hopeful but delusional old bat."

"She told me you're struggling with the guilt."

"Marissa... I don't know why you're talking to my mother in the first place. But I can assure you that Ember is doing just fine. She's getting stronger each day. And yes, I've gotten her a therapist to help navigate the waters, but we are far from talking mental hospital."

She looks down at their manicured nails in what I can only assume is disappointment.

"I'm sorry if you thought that opened a door for you," I say much harsher than intended.

She looks up at me with tears in her eyes. "I'm struggling here too, you know. Do you even care about that?"

"Of course I do," I say, softening my voice. "But I've been honest and straightforward with you, Marissa. I'm sorry. We are over... and will *always* be over. Maybe I should have said the last sentence to you earlier. I'm sorry."

"There's going to be a day Ember won't be with you. She's unstable. It doesn't take a therapist to see that. We all see it. Everyone around you sees it. And we all see you are still held captive. You haven't truly escaped yet. I want to be there for you, but I can't just stand here and watch this." She takes a step toward the door and then looks over her shoulder at me. "I wish you luck, Christopher. Based on what your mother has told me... you're going to need it."

She leaves, but the door is still left open. Before I can get up to close it, Max enters his office. "You okay, man? Marissa looked pretty pissed."

"Yeah," I say, walking from behind his desk and sitting on the nearby couch. I run my fingers through my hair and sigh. "How did my life get so damn complicated? What did I do to deserve this? My karma is fucked."

Max goes and sits down at his desk, shaking his head. "I wouldn't want to walk a day in your shoes; that's for sure." He leans back in his chair and begins rocking casually. "You sure you're up to getting back to work so soon?"

"Yeah, I need to. I have another person to be responsible for."

Max rolls his eyes. "Whatever, Christopher *Davenport*. I don't think you're exactly hurting for money."

"You know I don't touch that money," I say as I sigh. "But I'm getting tempted to. I'm struggling to find a place for Ember and me to buy. At least a place that doesn't require me to touch the trust."

"If you need some time off, just let me know. I think the fact that you were held captive in a basement by a serial killer earns you some personal days."

I chuckle, trying to shake off my bad mood.

"Marissa isn't handling Ember well, is she?" he asks.

"I don't blame her for feeling the way she does," I say. "But I can't change what happened."

"Do you want to? Change it?"

I pause to consider the question. "Actually, no. I mean, it's not like I wanted to be married. I may have never gotten married. But now that I have Ember, I don't want to change it. I know that might seem crazy, but it feels like we belong. Like we were meant to be."

"I get it," Max says with a nod. "When do I get to meet this girl?"

"Soon," I reply. "I've been really careful not to throw too much at her. The media insanity really made things tougher to get acclimated than I wanted. I mean, the girl hasn't ever lived. She's been locked up in a ghost town her entire life. So many things that you and I take for granted is all new for her. I forget that sometimes and am reminded when I see her wide eyes take something in for the first time."

"I can't imagine what's that like. What about you? Did all of that fuck with your head? PTSD and stuff? Nightmares?"

I pause before answering. Part of me wants to lie and tell him all is fine, but I've always been straightforward with Max. "I have nightmares. Not as many as Ember does, but I still dream about Richard, the cellar, and the acid pits. The couple I watched die still haunts me. I've gotten a therapist to help Ember and me work through it. He says it will take some time, and I know that. It fucking sucks sometimes, though. I wish I could speed up time so the healing could be done with."

"I'm not worried about you. You're one of the strongest motherfuckers I know. But do you ever worry about Ember? I mean... I can't imagine how someone can bounce back after what she's been through."

"She's getting stronger day by day. I worry about her... maybe too much. But she has a fighting spirit."

"Did that Richard fucker... rape her?" He cringes the minute he asks the question. "Sorry... that may be too personal."

"He's a sick fucker, but no, he didn't rape her. When we had sex on our wedding night, she was a virgin. Although the asshole forced all that to happen, so yes, rape in its own way."

"Sorry, man. Jesus, it's really unbelievable."

"And yet Ember is the most loving and open woman I've ever met. She's broken in many ways, which is understandable, but she doesn't hold back on her feelings. She's free with them. It's refreshing to have someone who doesn't play all the mind games or manipulate. It's not in her makeup. She's genuine and true. I'm in awe every day with how she looks at things. She doesn't see herself as a victim, which I find admirable."

"You look healthier," Max says. "I expected you to be a waif of a man, beaten, and scarred."

"I am healthier. My life is back on track. I have focus now. That, and I'm done drinking and popping pills nonstop. I like being sober. Fucked up that something like being hit upside the head by a killer had to do it for me, but regardless, it's one of the good things that came from this nightmare."

Max looks at his computer and types on his keyboard. "Okay, well, I emailed you your schedule for the next month. It's full. So if you ever feel it's too much, you just tell me. Don't feel you have to stress you or Ember out over it. I can find substitutes."

"I can handle it," I say. "I want to work. I need to work. It's the one area I feel I have complete control of right now." I smirk. "That, and I'm homeless."

Max laughs. "A Davenport homeless. That's a good one."

19

Dr. Stevens thinks I'm improving, and I have to agree.

He's helping me realize that Papa Rich— Richard is not and has never been my father. Hallelujah Junction is not my home, and therefore, I can stop missing it, or at least can start the process in saying goodbye to that part of my life. But he also allows me to grieve everything without feeling ashamed for it. He tells me the feelings and thoughts I'm having are normal. He makes me feel... sane.

Walking out of the bathroom, drying off my hair with a towel, I'm excited for the evening. Christopher has promised to take me to Luciano's for dinner, and I'm looking forward to seeing our friends again. Getting dressed in one of my favorite dresses from Christina's, I decide I want to ask Louisa if she has any makeup I can borrow. Maybe she'll offer me some tips. I haven't really put makeup on yet, unless you count lip gloss, and I think tonight will be as good as any night to start.

I walk toward Louisa's room and stop. I hear something. Whispers.

Whispers from downstairs.

I know Ms. Evans is still here, and I know Louisa is in her room getting ready for her own social engagement. But the murmurings are male. Though I can't hear what's being said, it's masculine. And it's clearly whispers. Whoever is downstairs is purposely trying to keep their voices concealed.

My heart stops, and I don't know why. I shouldn't be concerned. I shouldn't be worried.

Tiptoeing to Louisa's double doors, I try to turn the handle. I don't want to knock in case the people below hear me. Why I care if they hear me or not, I'm not sure, but something in my gut tells me to be quiet.

Louisa's door is locked.

I glance down the hallway at my door and consider running back to my room and locking myself inside. But I feel silly. Why am I afraid? Why am I assuming the worst?

The whispers stop, and I freeze, listening.

Darting my eyes to the top of the stairs, I see a piece of straw, and then another. In fact, there is straw in several places along the landing and near a table that has a collection of glass vases on display. I run over to the table to see the straw closely.

Dr. Stevens would tell me that I'm creating the straw in my mind due to the trauma, but as I pick up the dry fiber and run it in between my fingers, I know I'm not making it up.

The whispers...

The straw...

They're here.

I pick up a vase and hold it as a weapon. If they're going to try to kidnap me, I'm going to put up a fight. I won't go willingly. I won't leave Christopher. I won't let them hurt him, or Louisa, or Ms. Evans. I look over the railing to see if I can tell who is down

there. I now know there are men down there. I
know. I know!

I need to be strong. I need them to know I'm not
weak; I'm not someone they can mess with.

Not thinking but acting on the need to rid them
from my life, I toss the glass vase over the stair
railing to the foyer down below.

"Get out of this house now!" I scream as the shards
of glass shoot in all directions as it crashes down
below.

When I don't hear footsteps running away, or even
see bodies running out the door, I reach for
another vase and throw it down below.

"I said get out! Get out!"

"What are you doing?" Louisa screams. "My vases!
Stop! Ember, what in the world are you doing?"

I see Ms. Evans run to the bottom of the stairs,
terror in her eyes as she looks at Louisa and me.
She pauses for a moment but then charges up the
stairs.

"What are you doing?" Louisa asks as she
approaches cautiously.

"They're downstairs!"

Louisa looks at Ms. Evans, who is just now at the top of the stairs. "Do we have guests?"

Ms. Evans shakes her head. "No one is here, Ember. It's just the three of us."

"I heard men speaking downstairs. I heard them."

"There are no men in this house, for Christ's sake. You've lost your mind," Louisa says, clearly upset about her priceless vases.

But she should care about her life! Not the vases.

"You both aren't listening to me. No one is listening to me! I heard them. I can feel them!"

"No one is here, Ember," Ms. Evans says calmly with her hands out to try to placate me.

"I'm not making this up!" I scream. "It's not in my head!"

But maybe it is.

Maybe I am crazy.

Maybe Dr. Stevens hasn't been helping me at all.

Maybe....

Ms. Evans runs past Louisa and tries to reach for my hand as I grab another vase and throw it against the wall as I scream to the world. Rage fills me. A pure, uncontrollable rage. Why? Why did this happen to me? Why did Papa Rich do this to me? Why do I have to live in New York hating every day that passes because I feel like a stranger in my own body and in my own existence?

I don't belong here!

I don't belong!

"She's lost her goddamn mind," Louisa shouts as she reaches in her pocket for her phone. I know she's going to call Christopher.

"Stop!" I scream as I lunge for the woman's hand. "Don't you call him! Don't you dare!"

The ringing in my ears won't stop. The voices are getting louder. They're screaming at me to leave. To run far away and never look back. The straw is here. *They* are here.

But maybe I want them to be.

Maybe I want to run *to* them instead of away.

Maybe I want to beg for forgiveness and hope Papa Rich will take me back.

Is that crazy?

Yes, that's fucking crazy!

"Ember," Ms. Evans says with an even voice as she takes a cautious step toward me. "Calm down. It's just us. Calm down. Everything's going to be okay."

I can see Ms. Evans is scared. So is Louisa. I don't blame them. I'd be scared of me too. But they should be so much more terrified of who is lurking in the shadows of this house. Papa Rich will kill them both for keeping me in this house. In his eyes, he'll see it as the ultimate sin. They will pay.

"You better run," I warn. "He's here." I pick up another glass vase and hold it like a weapon, ready to attack. "If he finds you, if he finds you both, you're dead."

"No one's here," Ms. Evans says calmly. "It's just the three of us." She tries to reach for the vase, but I only lift it higher and angle my body so she can't. "You don't need that vase. You're safe."

Louisa takes this opportunity to dial her phone. She takes several steps away from me and calls Christopher. I know she is. And good. He needs to be here. Not to protect me, but to protect *them*.

"Look," I say, bending down to my knees and pulling the pieces of straw from the broken glass. "Straw!" My finger is bleeding from cutting it on the glass, which drips off the straw. "You see it now, don't you? Straw!"

Louisa screams into the phone. "She's holding a vase, ready to hit us. She told us to run and that we're in danger. She's breaking all the vases and screaming. Christopher, she's out of control. Hurry! Hurry! She's going to hurt us."

I'm not going to hurt them. Not me. But yes, they are in danger!

20

EMBER

"GO TO OUR ROOM NOW!" CHRISTOPHER SHOUTS AS he points to the stairs.

"You don't understand! They're here! They're here!"

"You're out of control!"

"Listen to me. He's here! Or at least he was!"

Christopher marches toward me and places his hands firmly on my shoulders. "Ember, listen to me. I just searched this house from top to bottom. There is no one here! No one has ever been here. This is all in your head. Do you hear me?" He's screaming now. He's shaking me as tears run down my face and my heart beats out of my chest. "You are losing your mind and bringing me to the loony bin with you!"

"You have to listen to me—"

"I warned you, Christopher," Louisa interrupts. "I told you that the girl needs help. Serious mental help that we aren't equipped to handle here. She's needs to be committed. She needs to be put away, so she doesn't hurt herself or someone else."

I spin on my heels, breaking free from Christopher's hold. "Shut up! Shut up!" I hate her words. I hate that she is telling my husband I need to be away from him. "Shut up!" My screech is so loud and high-pitched that I wonder if it will shatter the vases I haven't managed to ruin.

Christopher takes hold of my upper arm and shakes me. "Our room, now! Ember, I swear to God, go to our room!"

Louisa has her hand on her chest and acts like I punched her. I want to punch her. I do. How dare she tell my husband I need to leave him and that he needs to leave me? How dare she?

"I have a very important party to be at tonight," Louisa says as she fans her face. "How am I expected to function when I have a madwoman living under my roof?"

I look up to Christopher's dark eyes and consider engaging further but decide we need to talk in private. So rather than saying another word, I charge to our room and throw myself on the bed, crying in rage, fear, and frustration.

There's no way I'm imagining this. I saw the straw. Why would there be straw in the house? But I also know how this looks to Christopher.

"Why can't you at least try?" Christopher booms as he charges into the room, wild eyes, fury etched in every feature.

I scurry back against the headboard, hating that he's so angry.

"I can't be here all the time, Ember! You have to understand that. I have a career. I have to earn for our futures. I need you to be able to stand on your own two feet while I'm gone. I can't deal with the insanity. Why can't you give me that?"

"He was here!" I shout, the sound foreign to my own ears. "I saw the straw. He has Scarecrow either with him or doing his bidding. I saw the straw! I'm not making this up. I'm not losing my mind. I told you from the beginning that he would never let me go. You think I'm safe here, but I'm not. Not from him. Not ever."

Christopher crosses the room to me, hands fisted and rage in his eyes. "Do you hear yourself? I need you to be strong, Ember. I'm trying to be patient. I'm trying to understand what you went through."

"What I'm going through now is far worse than anything I endured in Hallelujah Junction." I instantly regret my words and wish I could take them back, but they're out, and I might as well be honest now. "I feel like I'm in a prison. Like I'm in shackles on display for all to judge me. I'm the freak from the ghost town, who poor Christopher feels he has to take care of. You think I don't hear? You think I don't see? I know what I am to your mother and your friends."

"Then stop acting like a freak!" he screams.

His words feel like a punch to the gut or a blow to the face. I know his mother thinks I'm a freak, but Christopher? Does he?

He begins to pace the room back and forth like a caged animal. And a caged animal is clearly what he is, and I'm the keeper of the key.

"My mother said you started screaming hysterically and throwing her priceless vases. Explain to me why you did that." His voice is calmer, but he hasn't stopped pacing, and his face is growing redder by the minute.

Of course his mother painted my actions in the worst light.

"I screamed when I saw the straw. I thought I heard Scarecrow and Papa Rich whispering down below. I felt he was near... maybe with Papa Rich. I picked up a vase for protection, and I... I didn't just purposely throw the vases around. I would never do that."

"My mother said both she and Ms. Evans saw no sign of straw anywhere. No sign that anyone had entered the house. You have them both in a near panic now, thinking some one-legged man has broken into the house. My mother had to take medication to calm herself down."

"I didn't mean to scare them," I say as I look down to my hands trembling in my lap. "But he was in the house, Christopher. I know he was."

He takes a deep breath and then exhales. He does this a couple of times with his back to me before turning around and slowly walking to the bed. He sits down, and I flinch as he does, preparing for a punishment of some sort.

He notices my cowering. "Why did you just flinch? Do you really think I'd hit you?"

"You're angry with me," I say softly.

"Yes. But that doesn't mean I'd hit you. I'm not Richard."

"I know you aren't him, but I've also never seen you so mad at me."

I know deep down Christopher would never really hurt me on purpose, but then at the same time, there have been times I don't recognize the man in front of me. It's like there is a passing sun over him. Sometimes, he's in the shade, and other times, the sun is beaming on his handsome face. Sometimes dark and sometimes light.

He reaches for my hand and closes his eyes for several moments before looking at me with such sadness. "I'm frustrated. Extremely frustrated. But not just at you. I know this hasn't been easy on you, and it sure as fuck hasn't been easy on me. I'm trying to do the best that I can. I understand you're afraid. I'm trying to be sensitive to that fact, but you have to stop with the Scarecrow and Papa Rich talk. If not for your own sanity, then for everyone's around you."

I want to argue. I want to shake some sense into him and make him see the truth. Scarecrow is out there. Papa Rich is out there. They are waiting and watching, and Christopher is too blind to prepare for the attack. And an attack is most definitely coming. But Christopher has just started to calm down, and I don't feel like continuing down the path of fury any longer.

"I'm having a hard time letting go of my past. I'm having a hard time accepting my future," I confess. "And I know you say you love me, but I feel like I'm a burden or an obligation. I can't help it."

"You aren't either of those to me," Christopher states firmly. His jaw is locked again, and his brow furrows. "Have I not shown my devotion to you? My commitment? I don't take either of those lightly. And I've been working my ass off to try to get our lives started. I wish it could all happen overnight, but it can't."

"I don't want to be left alone anymore. The walls are closing in on me here. You go off to work and to work events in the evenings, and I'm here, alone." I'm changing the subject from Papa Rich, but this is another issue I feel I need to address. "I stare out our bedroom window just like I stared out the window of the schoolhouse. Nothing has changed. I'm still a ghost just haunting a different place."

"I have to for my work, and the only reason I haven't taken you to the evening dinners and parties is that I'm worried you aren't ready. It's a lot of people. A lot of questions."

"But I want to. I'm your wife. I want to be by your side. I have to start figuring out this new way of living. I need to stop being the 'freak' everyone thinks I am."

He circles his fingertip on my hand again, which I'm realizing is something that gives me comfort. "Fair enough," he says. "I can't keep you locked up in a gilded cage safe and protected forever."

I almost want to scream out that I'm not safe. Far from it. Scarecrow and Papa Rich are here! But I stay quiet. I need more proof. I need to wrap my head around the hows and the whys before I try to make people believe me. I can't keep saying my *gut* or because I *feel* they are.

"Tomorrow night, there's a party at a politician's penthouse. He's trying to get donations for his campaign and to earn goodwill. I normally wouldn't go to something like this, as it's pretentious, arrogant, and everything I'm against. But I promised my editor I would, and I'm trying to prove in my own way that I'm also not the 'freak' some people think I am now." He moves a little closer to me and pulls me into his arms, holding me close. "Let's go tomorrow as husband and wife."

I snuggle in close to him, pressing my face to his chest and inhaling his essence.

"I'm sorry I lost my cool," he says as he begins petting my hair softly.

"I'm sorry I angered you. I'm also sorry I broke all those vases. I'm sure they were really expensive. I owe your mother an apology at the least."

"My mother will be just fine. It's not like she hasn't had her bout with hysterics a time or two."

"I still shouldn't have broken what isn't mine. I was scared. I know you feel I shouldn't be. But I was. I just don't want you to think... less of me. I don't want you to think I'm a freak."

"I love you, Ember. I truly do. I've never been good at knowing or showing what that exactly means... love. But I know it's something I feel for you."

As if he just released a flood gate, I cry. I can't help it. "I love you too. I don't know what that looks like either or how it's supposed to feel. I've been told all my life how it should be and how it should feel. Love confuses me. I thought I loved Papa Rich. I still sometimes think I do. But then I met you. And I'm with you now, and... this is what love is supposed to feel like. How I feel right now in your arms."

He presses his lips to mine and kisses me with more passion than ever before. It's like the kiss is needed to repair what we may have broken. It's a kiss to bandage the wounds inside.

"You're my wife," he mumbles into my hair.

"You're my husband."

"I want to fuck you," he states so simply.

"I want you to fuck me."

How we can go from yelling to tears to wanting to fuck, I have no idea. But I want Christopher inside me, tearing and clawing his way in as he does it.

"Hard," he whispers. "I want the tears staining your face right now to be from how hard and deep I'm going to fuck you. No longer out of sadness or fear."

"Yes," I breathe out, wanting something more raw and primal. "Punish me. You may not hit me. You may not beat me. But I want my husband to punish me *his* way. I want there to be consequences for what I did... bad, bad consequences." I playfully wink as I lean forward and kiss him again. "Your wife has been a bad girl."

"Ember," he moans as he begins yanking and pulling at my clothes.

He doesn't take his time. He doesn't let me help. He just strips me of my clothes like a beast would devour his prey. He stands up just long enough to unfasten his belt and to pull it from the loops. The swishing sound sends a shiver down my spine, and I fear he's going to belt me and truly discipline me, but before I can allow any sense of panic to set in, he's reaching for my wrists, pulling them together, and fastening them tightly with the leather belt. Once he is standing naked in front of me, he pushes me back against the mattress, my bound wrists up above my head.

"I'm going to fuck you like I've always wanted to. Not easy. Not gentle. I'm not going to hold back. I'm going to make you cry. I'm going to make you scream. I'm going to make you forget everything except me. You will only be able to focus on my cock as I spread you wide. There's no one here tonight to hear you. There's nothing to hold me back. You're going to scream my name over and over again. It's time you're punished, Ember. It's high time I show you what happens when you piss off your husband."

He doesn't pause but mounts me like an animal out of control. His cock penetrates me without warning, and he's deep inside, pounding away with fervor. My body rocks beneath him, hands still bound above my head. He squeezes my breast and then lowers his head and nibbles the other. I'm already reaching climax, and he's only begun.

The force of his cock pumping in and out is bruising but so damn hot that I cry out as the first of what I know will be many orgasms washes over me.

"Christopher," I cry out, wanting so badly to cling to his back with my hands. I want to claw him. I want to mark his flesh with the signs of my pleasure, but I'm bound and at his mercy.

"That's right, baby. Come around my cock."

He continues to drive into me with aggression and primal need. He groans as he does so, and all I can do is lie there and allow him to do as he pleases to me. My legs are spread wide, my pussy even wider with his large shaft mastering my entrance, and my arms are cast above my head. I have no control, but I love that he's got it all. My Christopher. My husband. Mine.

I cry out loudly as another jolt of electricity sizzles through me. My body has no time to recover before Christopher continues with his relentless fucking. He was right when he said he would fuck me to tears of pleasure, because that is exactly what's happening. My body is alive. Fear is gone. Any insanity I experienced while shattering precious glass has been replaced with a new level of insanity.

A primal insanity.

An erotic insanity.

An insanity that I never want to be cured of.

When it comes to Christopher, I never want to be sane again.

"Come with me," he rasps as he lowers his hand to my clit and circles the sensitive area to where I have no choice but to oblige him in his request.

His deep moan of pleasure blends with my screams of completion, and any argument, any signs of displeasure from before, are vanquished. Just like that, we have healed the wounds... at least for now.

CINDERELLA.

I remember reading that story repeatedly, but never once did I ever think I would get to live the fairy tale myself. I now have my Prince Charming, and I also have my happily ever after... or at least we are working toward that.

But as I stand in my new dress that Christina found for me, wearing makeup she also taught me how to apply, I know I look like a princess.

"Gorgeous," Christopher says from behind me. He approaches and places his lips on my bare shoulder. "I may want to stay home tonight and keep you all to myself."

"Are you sure my dress isn't too black?" I ask, loving how the fabric and cut accentuates every curve of my body. *Seductive* was the word Christina used to describe it. But I wasn't used to wearing black.

"I may have to remove the dress just to show you how beautiful you are." He sighs. "But the car is waiting outside for us."

I giggle, and my face heats. Turning to face him, I kiss him on the lips before saying, "I'm ready."

He leads me downstairs and adds, "Remind me to thank Christina for all her help with getting you ready. You're stunning."

"She seemed different today," I say, remembering how she seemed to space out, not always hearing what I said. "Sort of sad."

"Michael is having some financial issues with Luciano's. I think they are both just going through a hard time. I know them, though; they'll get through it." He spins me around in a little dance when we reach the front door. "But tonight is all about you and me. I will have the most beautiful woman in the room by my side. I can't wait to show off my wife."

Not allowing myself to overthink or get myself worked up, I think of nothing else but what a fun time Christopher and I will have. Dr. Stevens told me in our session today to not always plan for the worst. To not think something bad will happen. If I focus on the good and the light, then I'll be able to fight off the bad and the darkness.

I am determined to listen.

My very first party, and although the number of people attending is more than Christopher is comfortable with for both of us, he's been nothing but supportive and encouraging of me attending. I feel welcomed and not a burden. I actually feel Christopher is proud to have me by his side.

When we walk into the building in what he tells me is in Manhattan, I'm surprised to see how large it is and even more shocked to find out the owner has converted several floors into his home. The party is on the main penthouse level, but we start on the first level and leave our coats in a room bigger than the schoolhouse of Hallelujah Junction. I thought Louisa's house was large, but it's nothing in comparison to where we are now.

"If you ever feel uncomfortable or want to leave, you just tell me. We'll leave whenever you want to," Christopher says as we choose to take the stairs to the penthouse rather than waiting for the elevator with some other guests.

"I don't want you to worry about me," I say. "I'll be fine. I want you to be able to network and do what you need to do for your career." I reach for his hand and squeeze it. "I'm a big girl. I can handle myself. I need to start sometime if I want to be married to the famous *Rolling Stone* photographer who is in such demand."

Christopher rolls his eyes as he opens the door to the party. The sound is intense at first, but I quickly shake off any nerves it causes.

"Let's get a drink," he says, leading me hand in hand to a bar near a huge floor-to-ceiling window that overlooks the entire city. The lights of the skyline and all the buildings are absolutely stunning and nearly take my breath away. "Yeah, this place has one of the best views in New York."

"I've never seen anything like it. It's gorgeous." I look around the penthouse as Christopher orders our drinks and soak in the opulence.

All the furniture is white, and the only color is in the bright artwork hanging on the walls. Huge chandeliers hang from above that sparkle right along with the city views that master the room, since huge windows surround the entire penthouse. Music is playing faintly, but the constant hum of the people milling around really creates the melody of the room. There are so many faces I don't recognize, and yet no one seems to pay any attention to Christopher and me. We're blending in with everyone else, which is odd but refreshing. I'm so used to having all eyes on me, but right now, at this party, they're anything but.

"No one is staring," I tell Christopher as he hands me a glass of white wine.

"Yeah, the one nice thing about attending parties of this caliber is the people in the room are celebrities, power players, socialites, criminals, or politicians. Everyone has their own story and their own spotlight. We are just another star shimmering in the sky here."

"I like it."

We spend the next couple of hours moving from one grouping of people to the next. I never realized just how charming and personable Christopher is, but he truly impresses me with his ability to work a room, never once leaving my side or making me feel like I didn't belong. And he was right in saying we were just another star in a sky full of them. Aside from an occasional question or mention of how they heard of me, the topic of conversation seemed to stay away from my former life and my serial killer father.

I'm pleasantly surprised when I see Christina at the party. Last I spoke to her, she wasn't sure if she and Michael would be attending. She didn't want to come without him, and she wasn't sure if he'd be able to break free from the restaurant.

Christopher is still in heavy conversation with a man about stocks or something of that nature, so I politely excuse myself for a minute and walk over to my friend.

"You came," I say as I approach.

She smiles but doesn't seem her usual self as she does. "Michael and I decided to come after all."

I look around for her husband but don't see him anywhere. "Where is he? I want to say hello."

Christina shrugs and reaches for a flute of champagne being carried on a tray by a waiter. "Who knows. Drinking with friends or something."

It's not hard to see she isn't exactly pleased with her husband. I decide to try to cheer her up by saying, "You look pretty. I love your dress."

She glances down and then chuckles. "Glad someone noticed." She takes a deep breath, a large drink from her champagne, and then adds, "Okay, I'm shaking off my bad mood. No need to ruin a party." I watch her paint on a new smile—a fake one—but regardless, she does appear to be shaking off her mood. "Where's Christopher?"

I point in his direction. "I've met some really interesting people since being here. The party's fancier than I'm used to, but I don't feel nearly as out of place as I was expecting."

"I'm glad you're having a good time," she says.

"I am, but if you'll excuse me, I'm going to go use the restroom."

I find where one is and see a small line waiting outside to use it. I take my place, feeling a little uneasy as all the other women seem to know each other and are talking. They clearly came to the bathroom as pairs or threesomes. I wish I had convinced Christina to come with me now, but I didn't realize going to the bathroom was a group effort.

Standing by myself, trying not to stare at anyone, and hoping I look casual and confident, I see Marissa approach me. I haven't noticed her before at the party, nor did I know she'd be attending, but then again, there are so many people that I can see how that's possible.

"Hello, Ember," she says with a smile.

The friendly greeting doesn't seem genuine, but I reply just as sweetly with "Hi, Marissa. Nice to see you." I hate lying. It's not nice to see her. My stomach dropping and my palms sweating prove that fact.

"I've been worried about you. How have you been since your *incident*?" she asks, not quietly, so anyone around can hear if they want to.

"What incident?" I have no idea what she's talking about.

"I was with Christopher in LA when his mother called us about you having your... incident."

"Wait... what?" A ringing begins in my ears, and bile forms in the back of my throat. "You were in LA with Christopher?"

I can't breathe.

I can't breathe.

She nods and replies as if it's only natural she'd be with Christopher. "We were at our favorite pub when the call came in. We were both so worried about you. With everything you've been going through, it's so kind of Christopher to be there helping you work it out." She reaches out and pats my arm. "Christopher and I are *both* here for you. You can count on me too."

I inhale deeply, but air doesn't seem to enter my lungs. I scan the room for my husband but don't see him. I want to puke, but the line for the bathroom isn't moving. All I know is I can't stand here any longer. Not with her.

Not with Marissa.

They were in California together. He was going to spend the night....

They were at their favorite place.

He's helping me out... so kind of him....

"Excuse me," I say as I push my way by her and storm out of the penthouse.

I need air.

I need to leave.

I need.... What the fuck do I need?

Running down the stairs to the coat room, I close the door behind me so I can have a minute to myself and gather my senses. I can't just go home. Home...? Where is my home?

Has Christopher been seeing Marissa the entire time? Is he just being nice to me and pretending to be my husband until I get mentally stronger? Is that why he's helping me learn how to be independent? Is his plan to leave me and be with Marissa the minute he feels I'm ready to be alone?

The door to the coat room opens, and Michael enters. "Ember? Are you okay? I saw you running in here. What's going on?"

He approaches me, and though I'm happy to see a familiar face, I can see his eyes are glossy, and he stumbles a bit as he walks to me. I smell heavy booze on his breath as he takes me into his arms in an embrace.

"I'm here," he adds. "Tell me what's wrong."

I try to wiggle free from his hug, but he holds me tightly against his chest. "I'm fine. I just want to go home."

"You don't seem okay," he murmurs into my hair.

I push my hands against his chest and am able to break the connection by taking two steps back toward the wall. "I need some space. It's a lot of people and activity upstairs, and—"

"Where's Christopher?" he interrupts, and he closes the distance between us, pushing me up against the wall of the room. Coats are now all around us, and even if someone came into the room, I doubt they would be able to see us behind all the furs and leathers.

"Can you please go upstairs and tell him I'd like to go home?" I ask, panic setting in as Michael is not backing away but pinning me against the wall instead with his hands on each side of me.

"Ah, you don't need to leave now." His breath is on my face. "Not when you are upset. Let me make you feel better."

Michael places his lips on my neck and begins assaulting my skin with wet kisses all over.

I try to push him away, but he's not budging. "Michael, stop. Stop!"

"Shh," he says as he moves his lips to my mouth and kisses. "You don't want someone to hear us. If Christina comes in and catches us, she'll be devastated. You don't want to do that to her, now do you? Not to your friend. And Christopher... what will he think if he catches us being intimate?"

"I don't want this," I say in a low voice, trying to turn my face away from his kiss, but he only pushes harder and with more force.

His hand lowers and finds the bottom of my dress. He lifts it out of the way and fingers the edge of my panties before I'm able to do anything. I try to take hold of his wrist, but nothing I do stops his advance.

"Michael, I think you've had too much to drink," I say as I do whatever I can to break free from his hold but can't fight off his strength. "Please don't do this. Christina and Christopher—"

"Will never know," he cuts in as he somehow lowers my panties to my thigh. "It will be our little secret."

His finger pushes past my folds and enters inside me. I gasp at the intrusion. Shame and fear make my knees weak, but I'm too paralyzed with indecision to fight him off. I want to scream for help, but I don't want Christina to know what her husband is doing. Michael's right in the fact that she'd be devastated. And what will Christopher do if he finds out his wife has another man's finger inside her pussy? He may never forgive me.

I can claw and punch, but then that can draw attention to the coat room as well. No, I have to handle this discretely. This has to be *our little secret*, like Michael said.

"Don't do this," I plead. "Michael, I'm asking you to stop. No one will have to know this happened. I won't tell anyone."

"Exactly," he says, pushing his lips hard against mine and pulling us to the ground. "No one has to know."

Within seconds, he's on top of me, lowering his pants. My dress is pulled up to my stomach, my panties down to my ankles now, and I know what's coming.

I push against his chest hard, considering gouging out his eyes, but before I can decide if I possess the internal fortitude to do so, he reaches for my hands and confines them up above my head. With his weight and strength, there is nothing I can do.

His penis is rubbing against my pussy, and he's trying to find the hole to enter. His dick isn't hard, so he's having a hard time at finding his way inside.

"Michael, think of Christina," I say as tears run down my face, soaking my hair. "Your wife. Think what your wife would think. And Christopher. He's your friend. Don't do this. It's not you. Please don't do this. Christina, Christina, Christina," I begin chanting.

He freezes, his limp cock resting against my violated sex. He lowers his face to my hair and begins to cry.

"Don't say her name. Don't."

"Christina," I say again. "Think of what this will do to Christina."

"I'm so fucked up," he murmurs. "I'm so fucked up."

I take this opportunity of his weakness and use it to my advantage. I'm able to push him off me, springing to my feet as I pull up my panties and lower my dress. I look down at him, still lying on the ground with his pants lowered, sobbing. I consider kicking his ribs. I think about beating him over and over again. But rage doesn't exist inside me. Only sadness. I'm sad for him, I'm sad for me, I'm sad for all. I should hate him, but I don't. I should want vengeance, but I don't possess it.

We all sin.

We all fail.

He's no different.

Evil is everywhere.

I leave him where he's at and grab my coat as well as Christopher's.

I bolt out of the coat room without saying a single word and see Christopher exiting the elevator.

"Hey, where did you go? I've been looking all over for you," he says with a look of concern—or maybe annoyance. I can't tell.

"I'm ready to go home," I say, lifting the coats I'm carrying to show him. "I was just going get you."

"Is everything all right?" He approaches and takes his coat, puts it on, and then assists me in putting on mine as a true gentleman would.

A true gentleman who is taking secret trips with Marissa.

He leans in and kisses me on the cheek. His breath smells like Michael's, and I cringe.

Christopher notices and worry darkens his eyes. "Did something happen? You're acting differently than earlier."

I can't tell him about Marissa. I don't want to tell him what Michael just did. What good would come out of either? I don't want to face my demons anymore. I want to slink back into the shadows where it's safe.

"I'm just ready to go home."

22

EMBER

"What's going on with you?" Christopher asks as we sit in the back of the town car taking us home. "Did something happen at the party?"

I shrug as I watch the passing scenery whirl by faster than my eyes can adjust and take it all in.

"You went to the bathroom and never came back. Did something happen?"

I don't know how to tell Christopher the truth. Do I just blurt out that I found out he cheated on me with Marissa and then was nearly raped by one of his best friends? Would he even believe me if I told him? And if I tell him what I know about Marissa, will he finally confess and tell me he's been waiting for the right time to leave me? Will it be over?

I'm not ready for it to be over.

"I had a really good time." Which isn't a lie. I did at first. "I just got a little overwhelmed by it all at one point. That's it. I'm not used to so much so fast."

Christopher remains quiet for several minutes. I wonder if he's believing a word I say.

"I have a surprise for you," he finally says as we pull up to the house. "If you aren't too tired, I'd like to show you."

I want to crawl in bed and try to forget this awful night, but I can also see the excitement in Christopher's eyes, and I don't want to disappoint him.

"Surprise?" I ask, working harder than ever to paint a fake smile on my face.

He helps me out of the car and into the house. "Shh," he says. "I don't want anyone to wake up and be part of this surprise. It's going to just be our secret. It's going to just be our secret for as long as we can keep it that way."

Michael's words flood in, and I feel as if I'm going to vomit. *Our secret.*

"Ember," Christopher says, snapping me back into reality. "You okay. You seem... off."

I give the fake smile again and hold his hand as reassurance for him as well as for me. I need his strength to get me to put one foot in front of the other.

Is this what it feels like when your life is crashing all around you?

Christopher leads us up the stairs and then down to the end of the hallways. He then pulls a string to a hatch in the ceiling, opening it to a staircase.

"An attic?" I say.

"Yes, but more." He climbs the ladder and then turns around to extend his hand to me.

We enter the attic full of dust and boxes. We don't stay long, however, as he leads me to double doors made of glass. When he opens the doors, we step out onto a rooftop terrace. Strings of lights are hanging above us from the tip of the roof to the railing. It's like a curtain of stars.

"I know you've mentioned how you feel the walls are closing in on you a few times," Christopher begins. "And I know we have this terrace that's never been used, or at least in my adult life. So, I've been working on having it fixed up for you."

He leads us farther out, and I can see patio furniture displayed around a fire pit, pots of flowers, and plants all around. Trellises of ivy cover the walls, and little animal and gnome statues are tucked away in the corners. There's even a water fountain to help drown out the sounds of the city.

"I wanted you to have an outdoor spot that is just yours. A place for you to get out of the house. At least until I find us a place of our own. And I promise I'll give you an outside environment just like this, if not better, when we do move."

I turn to face him, tears rushing from my eyes, and I burrow my face into his chest and cry. I sob so loudly that I can hear myself over the fountain and the bustling soundtrack of New York.

"Hey," he soothes as he rubs my back and kisses the side of my head. "Why is this making you cry?"

I keep crying until my sobs turn to hiccups and my hiccups turn to ragged breaths as I try to regain my composure. Christopher allows me to cry, holding me closely, kissing me, rubbing circles on my back, and simply being there for me. When I finally calm down, he brings me to a two-man chaise lounge and lowers me onto it, then sits beside me. We are overlooking the city now, and the view distracts me from my anguish.

"Okay," he says softly. "Are you ready to tell me what has you so upset?"

I nod as I wipe at my nose. "I saw Marissa at the party," I begin.

I feel Christopher's body tense. "I didn't know she'd be there. I'm sorry. Did something happen?"

I like that we are sitting side by side. I don't have to look him in the eyes as I say, "She told me she was with you in LA. That you guys were together at your favorite place when Louisa called, asking you to come home because of me."

Christopher sits up straight and twists his body so he's facing me. "Whoa, this is not what it sounds like. I did not go to LA with Marissa."

My lip quivers as I say, "Please don't lie to me, Christopher. That's all I ask. Don't lie."

"I'm not lying," he says with more passion and conviction than I'm used to seeing. "I swear to you. I was in LA, and Marissa showed up. I had no idea she was going to come. It was a complete surprise. I swear." When I don't respond but rather narrow my eyes instead, he adds, "I know how this looks. Hell, I'm sure it's how Marissa wants it to look, but I did not have a getaway with her. That was the first time I had seen her since we first got back, and it was a complete surprise."

"You didn't go have drinks with her at your favorite place?" I ask, unsure if I believe Christopher or not. I've never known him to lie to me, but it doesn't make sense how this all could just be a misunderstanding.

He lets out a deep breath. "We had drinks at *my* favorite bar. I always go there when I'm in LA. And we only went to talk. I felt I owed her that. She deserved to have closure, since I had been avoiding her. That's all it was."

"She made it sound like you guys went together and that you were sitting there trying to figure out a way to help me. As a couple. You and her... a couple." I begin to cry again. I can't help it, and I'm surprised I even have tears left.

Christopher takes my chin between his fingers and pulls it up so I have to look into his eyes, which do appear to be sincere. "Never, Ember. Never. I told her I love you, and I do. I told her I want you as my wife, and I do. I made it very clear my intentions are to be with you and always you. I need you to believe that. I need you to have faith in that."

I break free from his hold and look away. "Why would she lie? Why would she tell me the things she did if they weren't true?"

"Because sometimes hurt people do mean things. And that's all this is. She's hurt, and she wants you to hurt too. She doesn't want us to be together and was trying to cause trouble. I'm sorry, Ember. I'm sorry you had to believe I would do that to you for even a second." He leans forward and kisses me softly. "Please tell me you believe me."

"I want to. But a part of me wonders if you're just saying what I want to hear. If you're too scared to tell me your true feelings."

"I'm not going to lie to you, Ember. I'm not. Yes, I'm guilty of not telling you things in order to protect your feelings, and I know it's wrong. I don't give you credit for being as strong as you are. I have to remind myself that you're the woman who helped me burn down a town and escape. There isn't a weak bone in your body. I'm sorry. I should have told you about Marissa earlier. Do you forgive me?"

I kiss him back as my answer.

I press my tongue into his mouth and swirl it around. I need the familiar taste, his touch, his smell. I consider telling him about Michael, but what will come of that? Christopher will rage and go after him. Christina will find out. And secretly, each person involved will blame me. No, it's not my fault, but they will. How could they not?

Michael and Christina could be over because of it. And maybe Michael deserves it to be over. But does Christina deserve to have her entire life destroyed?

And though I don't think Christopher would blame me or think I truly wanted any part of it, I wonder if it will just be one more thing that makes me a victim in his eyes.

Again.

I don't want to be a victim over and over again.

I'm fucking tired of being weak.

I'm tired of the damn tears.

I don't want to be afraid and in need of a Prince Charming to save me.

Life is fucking tough. The real world isn't a fairy tale. And I need to learn that. I need to deal with it. I need to survive it. *I* need to. Me. Not anyone else.

So, no. I won't tell anyone about Michael. How I choose to handle that situation will be up to me. Me.

"Thank you," I finally say, breaking from the kiss. "It's beautiful up here. It's like a storybook, magical area. I love the fairy lights and the fountain. I love it all."

He smiles and looks around. "My mother is a damn vampire, so I'm not worried about her coming up here. It's all yours. I'll work on getting the attic cleaned up too so it's not so dusty for you when you do come."

"I needed this," I confess. "The room is getting to me, and the house... well, the house is your mother's. I needed this." I lean in to kiss him again. "You always seem to know the exact right thing to do for me."

Needing to end the night with the last touch on my body to be from my husband rather than Michael's drunken molestation, I swing my leg over his lap and mount him, lowering my lips to his again. I bring my hand to his zipper and free his cock from the restraints with a skill I'm happy to be gaining as my sexual experience increases. I like the power I have when it comes to sex. As I grip his dick, hear his gasp, and watch his eyes close, I savor the control I'm in.

"I love you," he growls as I begin rubbing my palm up and down the shaft. I'm watching his face as I do so.

"I know you do," I say, applying more pressure as I stroke. "And I love you."

And for a splitting moment, I wonder if love is enough. When the world is determined to keep you apart, can you fight off all the enemies? Papa Rich, Scarecrow, Louisa, Marissa, Michael... ghosts who haunt us to the brink of madness. Can we fight them off? Is it possible?

Christopher takes hold of my hips and gets ready to flip me over, but I stop him.

"No. I want to make you come." I tighten my grip on his cock. "Like this. I want to watch your face as you come in my hand." I lift his shirt up so I can see his bare chest and the ripple of his abs. "I want to see your cum spill all over your smooth skin."

His breath hitches, his head falls back, and with an open mouth, he moans. He's getting pleasure from me and no one else. It's just the two of us. No one else.

"God, that feels so good," he praises as his cock grows even harder and bigger in my ministrations.

I jack him off, watching every facial expression, listening to every sound of pleasure. I tighten, I loosen, I speed up, and I slow down. He's close, and I know it. I love it. He's going to do exactly what I want him to do.

I'm in control.

My choice.

My decisions.

I'm in control.

23

EMBER

IF I DON'T CHANGE, I'M GOING TO BE STUCK IN TIME.

I know this, and although I feel like I'm taking steps forward, there's always something that happens that pulls me back.

I see shadows.

I hear whispers.

I try to pretend they aren't there, but they are.

The ghosts of Hallelujah Junction still haunt me.

The Feds notified Christopher yesterday that there had been several sightings of Richard. In Nevada, in California, Wyoming, and now Virginia. He's getting closer and closer to New York, and I know why.

He's coming for me. And no matter how much Christopher reassures me that he isn't and that I'm perfectly safe, I know the opposite. Christopher's wrong in this case. So very wrong.

And then there is Louisa Davenport.

She hates me. I see it. She wants me to go crazy. I see her smile every time I get spooked or am uneasy. She takes pleasure in my fear, but I can't tell Christopher this. It's his mother. He loves her. He won't believe me on this either. But I know she's waiting for me to snap so she can send me away to a mental institute. I'm not blind. I see her waiting. Waiting.

And then there is Christina and Michael, who we haven't seen since the party, and I seriously doubt we will. How? How can I face either of them again?

I often think Louisa is right; I should move away and start over. Sometimes it seems as if it's the only option. Go and hide. Hide from everyone.

"We'll get your passport soon," Christopher says as he brings the last of his bags down the stairs. "I really wish you could go to London with me. But I'm swooping in and swooping out as soon as I'm done with the shoot. I didn't even book a hotel."

"You didn't have to do that," I say. "You can stay. I'll be fine."

"We'll go back there together and travel the entire area once we get the passport. I promise." He gives his bags a onceover to make sure he has all he needs. "I'll be back as soon as I can." He presses his forehead to mine, our lips so close. "Are you sure you're all right with me going?"

I pat his chest and smile. "Yes. Go take wonderful pictures, and don't worry about me."

I glance up the stairs and see Louisa looking down on us. Her face is solemn and eyes dark.

Christopher reaches for the back of my head and pulls me into a kiss. A tingle runs up my spine from the intensity, and I wish we didn't have an audience, or I'd let my hands explore as we kiss goodbye.

"I love you, Ember," he whispers as he breaks the kiss. "Don't ever forget that."

"Goodbye, Christopher. I love you."

He picks up his bags and leaves the house to meet the driver waiting on the stoop.

I don't wait to see him drive away but decide to head to my room instead. I don't want to be around

Louisa and her judging eyes. I definitely don't want to speak with her unless I have to. I hope she doesn't take this opportunity to have any more of her heart-to-heart talks with me.

No thank you. Hard pass.

No need to keep pretending. We both don't care for each other, and there is no point in continuing the façade. I hate lies, and I don't want to keep one up if I don't have to. And I no longer have to. I'm at peace with how the woman feels about me. I'm at peace.

I enter the room and freeze.

The skin on the back of my neck prickles. A whoosh of eerie silence surrounds me as I close my bedroom door.

Straw.

A lot of straw.

In the middle of the room is a cross made from nothing but straw. A Godly and haunting greeting from my past. There is no mistake. There is no way this is coincidence. And there is no way this is in my head.

I can run. I can scream. I can spin on my heels, lock myself in my room, and call the police.

I have so many options.

But truly, deep down, I know there is only one choice. I have to face my insanity head-on.

I notice a familiar object on the desk as well. An old hardback book of *The Secret Garden*.

I lift the book from the table and feel the weight in my hands. It's a story that has followed me here— from the schoolhouse.

I read the book over and over again growing up. So much so that the pages were worn thin in places and even tearing. So much so that I had to tape the book together in some places.

I flip through the book from the desk and stop on page 49. Page 49, which is held together with scotch tape. Just like I had taped page 49 of my book back in Hallelujah Junction.

It's the same book.

"Do you like the book?" I hear Louisa ask from behind me. I hadn't noticed her entering the room, but my nearing nervous breakdown can be blamed for that.

I turn to face her and run my finger over the tape. "This is mine from the schoolhouse." I look up at her, already fearing the answer to my question before I ask, "How did you get this?"

I had been trying to get out of the storm since leaving the only home I knew. Walking through the dark, I hoped so badly that I'd find the light. But as I stare at the woman before me and face the raging hurricane around me, I know there's no hope on weathering the storm.

"The straw," I say, pointing at the cross, seeing the truth for the first time. "You've always been the one behind the straw, right?"

She says nothing but simply smiles.

"Why? Did you want me to lose my mind? Did you want to scare me to the point of insanity? This was your plan all along, wasn't it?"

Her smile doesn't waver.

"Are Papa Rich and Scarecrow here? Do you know where they are?"

I need to know the answer. I need to know I hadn't been losing my mind the entire time. They had been lurking in the shadows, watching, tormenting, stalking me to the point of insanity. And Louisa... she played the cat-and-mouse game with them. Hadn't she?

Or does she want me to believe they are here simply by planting the straw herself?

"Tell me," I demand. "Do you know where they are? Or is this all a sick game? How did you get my book? Who left this cross of straw?"

Her sickly smile only grows bigger as she takes a step toward me. Not answering my questions I so desperately need answers to, she finally says, "You know what you have to do," she says. "If you love my son like you claim, then you know you have to leave him. He can't take care of you forever. He can't watch your every move. You'll suffocate him, drown him in the broken shards that will forever be your history. Have mercy on my son. I'm asking you to do that, even though I shouldn't have to. *You* know what's right."

"Did you do this?" I scream, feeling the room begin to spin. "Tell me what's going on! Tell me!"

"I need you to come with me downstairs," she says, hooking her finger at me to follow.

I'm paralyzed for a moment, but as if under a trance, I eventually follow.

As we reach the top of the stairs, my knees nearly buckle as I look down below. As insanity nears, I hear her say, "They're waiting for you."

. . .

THE END

Is there really such a thing as a Happily Ever After for two broken people? I guess we'll find out.

Be sure to see what's next for Christopher and Ember in **TAKEN BRIDE**.

CAPTIVE BRIDE:

You will take this bride.

To have and to hold from this day forward.

Till death do you part.

This will be your solemn vow.

You have no choice.

Trapped in a twisted and dark courtship with a secret woman who needs my strength to survive, I will be wed.

Walking the thin line between lunacy and reality, I am now the protector of my future captive bride.

So, I have no choice but to recite the vows.

I take thee.

In this arranged matrimony.

Until we are parted by death.

KEPT BRIDE:

My history is forbidden.

My story, dark and twisted.

My future decided.

I know I don't belong in this decadent world—his world.

Money, power, and dark secrets surround me now.

I submit to it all to be his perfect obedient wife.

They stalk my every move, watching me, judging me.

I'm in the same prison just with different guards.

But all I care about is him.

His eyes, his touch, his hold over me.

I'm forever his kept bride, even though they all try to steal me away.

TAKEN BRIDE:

Secrets must be kept.

Vows never broken.

Till death do us part...

Unless everything changes.

Captive in one life...

Kept in another...

Taken to now be the wife I am forced to be.

I'm hidden away to face a dark reality only a few can survive.

But I have a purpose now. I can be the good wife I strive to be.

But he still wants me.

He will hunt me down.

He will find me and take back what was stolen.

I will be his wife if he has to fight until the death to make it happen.

ALSO BY ALTA HENSLEY

Prima

Mr. D

Mafia Lullaby

Captive Vow

Naughty Girl

Bad Bad Girl

Delicate Scars

Bride to Keep

His Caged Kitty

Bared

Caged

Forbidden

For all of my books, check out my Amazon Page!

http://amzn.to/2CTmeen

ABOUT THE AUTHOR

Alta Hensley is a USA TODAY bestselling author of hot, dark and dirty romance. She is also an Amazon Top 100 bestselling author. Being a multi-published author in the romance genre, Alta is known for her dark, gritty alpha heroes, sometimes sweet love stories, hot eroticism, and engaging tales of the constant struggle between dominance and submission.

As a gift for being my reader, I would like to offer you a FREE book.

DELICATE SCARS

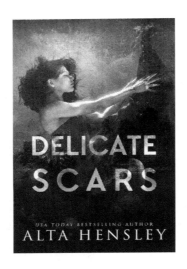

Get your copy now! ~

https://dl.bookfunnel.com/tnpuad5675

I was going to ruin her.

I knew it the moment I laid eyes on her. She was too naive, too innocent.

I would wrap her in the darkness of my world till she no longer craved the light... only me.

I should walk away, leave her clean and untouched... but I won't.

I hold her delicate heart in my scarred fist and I have no intention of letting go.

It all started with a book... doesn't that sound crazy?

For your entire world to come crashing down around you over research for a book?

But that is what it felt like the moment I met him.

My world tilted. Nothing made sense any more.

I only know he became like a drug to me... and I shook with need till my next fix.

Join Alta's Facebook Group for Readers for access to deleted scenes, to chat with me and other fans and also get access to exclusive giveaways:
Alta's Private Facebook Room

Check out Alta Hensley:
Website: www.altahensley.com
Facebook: facebook.com/AltaHensleyAuthor

Twitter: twitter.com/AltaHensley
Instagram: instagram.com/altahensley
BookBub: bookbub.com/authors/alta-hensley
Sign up for Alta's Newsletter: readerlinks.
com/l/727720/nl

Made in the USA
Las Vegas, NV
30 September 2021